# THE MAN AT KAMBALA

Sara lived with her father at Kambala in
Kenya and was accustomed to do as she
pleased there. She certainly didn't think
much of Steve York, the impossible man who
came to take charge in her father's absence.
'It's asking for trouble to run round a game
reserve as if it were a play park,' he told her.
Was Sara right to ignore him?

# THE MAN AT KAMBALA

*by*

KAY THORPE

MILLS & BOON LIMITED
17-19 FOLEY STREET
LONDON W1A 1DR

*First published 1973*
*This edition 1974*

© *Kay Thorpe 1973*

*ISBN 0 263 71554 X*

Made and Printed in Great Britain by
Cox & Wyman Ltd, London, Reading
and Fakenham

# CHAPTER ONE

THE crocodile lay half submerged in the mud – an island of mottled greens and browns which formed a perfect camouflage against the earth bank behind it. At the plop of the stone on the surface of the water it came suddenly and swiftly to life, sliding forward and under, dragging behind it a spike-ridged tail which seemed to go on for ever.

Sixteen feet if it was an inch, judged Sara from her vantage point on the far bank. Her largest yet.

She slid down and away from the grass-screened hollow and rolled over, brushing dust and debris from the front of her faded shirt and jeans with a careless hand. Then she sat for a moment looking out towards the distant sapphire-hued heights of the Mara Escarpment, allowing her eyes to drift down the rolling swell of the plains stretching away to the south. The Masai were setting their grass fires again; necessary to them to bring up new forage for their cattle, but sometimes too dangerously close to the track for comfort. Only last week her father had been forced to return to the station right through the middle of the crackling grass with the smoke practically smothering him. At least today the wind was in the other direction.

Her father would be on the plane now, heading for England. If his only brother hadn't died so suddenly, Sara doubted that he ever would have gone back. She herself had been only eight years old when they had come out here to East Africa, and could barely remember anything about her homeland. There had always been the intention of taking a holiday there one year, but somehow it had never quite materialized, and after her mother's death when she was twelve even the intention had faded into the never-never-land of one day. It was soon after this that her father's interest in wild life ecology had culminated in the offer of a position with the Game Department. Sara had still been at school when he had been posted to the Mara-Masai Reserve in charge of Kambala Station, and she had been forced to wait a whole six months before she was able to join him. She smiled, remembering the early days after her arrival. She had been so green, so unprepared for the vastness of it all. It had terrified her, and yet enthralled her. Now, three years later, it still enthralled her, but the terror had faded to respect. Out here there was a quality of time forgotten, a sharpening of the senses which gave every sight, every sound a clarity such as she had never experienced anywhere else. In three years she had made the four-hundred-mile round trip to Nairobi only once, and she had no particular desire to go again. Not yet, at any rate. This was her kind of life.

The sun was slanting fast. It was time to be getting back. She had told Ted that she wouldn't be gone longer than an hour. Not that he would worry about her if she was a bit late back. Like her father, he took it for granted that she knew enough by now not to take any risks. She reached for the gun lying in the grass at her side and came to her feet in one lithe movement, raking her fingers through her sun-bleached crop to get rid of any exploring insect life. She had left the Land-Rover parked just within the belt of forest edging the river. She made her way back to it along the narrow game trail by which she had entered, and reversed carefully out on to the track. She had seen what she had come to see, and that was always a good thought to take back with you. Kimani's largest croc to date was a fifteen-footer, although Ted claimed to have seen one approaching twenty. The trouble was that you never knew when he was serious. He could tell the tallest stories and have you believing them.

A couple of Masai were coming along the track on their way to the village beyond the ridge, long slender legs covering the ground smoothly, brown togas flying out behind. Sara slowed to pass them; there was the usual cordial exchange of *Jambos*, the flash of magnificent teeth, and they were past and gone. Tomorrow she must make the trip out to the village again. Mgari's third wife would have had her baby by now, and would be eager to show it off. This would be her fifth – or was it her sixth? Yet the girl couldn't be very much more than her own nineteen years. Kimani had said the other day that it wouldn't be long before the tribe began to think about moving on again. The pasturage within easy reach of the present *boma* was just about finished. Sara didn't want them to go, but she knew that it was inevitable. The Masai were no-madic by nature. One day they would all of them simply pick up their movable possessions and trek with their cattle until they found a suitable place to build a new home, and the huts they had left would stand empty until time and termites had reduced them to decay. There was a village just like that some ten miles away towards the Escarpment, abandoned before Sara had come here.

The track forked up ahead, the right hand going on towards the Escarpment, the left doubling back and up over a low ridge and into the trees. Sara took it cautiously, avoiding the potholes left from the last rains. It was always bad just here owing to the roots undermining the surface, and nothing very much could be done about those. She had got a wheel stuck once and had sat for a whole hour with a herd of elephant browsing within two hundred feet of her. Not that she had felt in any real danger. The wind had been in her favour, and like most wild animals the elephant seemed to regard a stationary vehicle without suspicion. There was a glint of water ahead of her, another loop of the same Mara river where she had watched the crocodile some twenty minutes ago. The track turned and ran parallel to the water for a few minutes, then switched back to emerge once more from the trees into a wide clearing sweeping up to the forty-foot bluff which protected Kambala from the rear.

The first time she had seen the station, Sara had not been overly impressed by the rambling, palm-thatched bungalow with its broad, shady verandas and shabby furnishings. Little had changed since then, she supposed. Still the same crop of outbuildings, the same wire enclosures. The orphanage was her own special project, although the only inmate at the moment was a tiny dik-dik fawn which Kimani had found beside its dead mother in the thicket above the river and brought back for her to nurse until it was old enough to fend for itself. At least that was the idea. Already it followed her around like a shadow whenever she let it out of the pen, watching her every move with those huge mouse eyes ringed in white. She had a feeling that the little creature would eventually join Kiki, her Sykes monkey, as a household pet rather than be turned out to take its chances on the plains.

Engrossed in her thoughts, she was almost at the house before she realized that the Land-Rover parked at the foot of the steps was not one of those belonging to the station, despite the Department's markings on the side. They hadn't been expecting her father's relief until the following day, but obviously he had managed to make it a day early. Sara drew up behind the other vehicle with a feeling of pleasant anticipation. She had met Bruce Madden when she had been in Nairobi with her father, and had liked him. Having him in charge for the six weeks of her father's leave wouldn't be at all bad.

She was half-way up the steps when a shout froze her in her tracks. Next minute Kiki came scampering through the doorway to leap into her arms and from there to her shoulder, where he sat chattering wildly and clutching hold of her hair with one paw while with the other he clasped a cigarette case to his skinny little chest. Close on his heels came a man in drill slacks and shirt who stopped abruptly at the sight of Sara standing there with the monkey hanging round her neck. In that long moment of suspended animation a pair of grey eyes went over her from head to toe and back again, openly appraising her slender young body and piquant features.

9

'Are you Dave Macdonald's daughter?' he demanded.

Something in his tone made her bristle. 'Yes,' she said shortly. 'If you've come to see my father he left for England yesterday.'

'I know that,' he said. 'What I can't understand is why you aren't with him. There was nothing said about his leaving you behind.'

She said slowly, 'I decided I didn't want to go. I don't suppose Dad saw any particular reason why he should inform the office that I was staying on at home. Isn't Bruce Madden coming?'

His eyebrows lifted faintly. 'No, he isn't. He had a bad attack of malaria and finished up in hospital. I'm Steve York.' He looked beyond her to the car she had just vacated. 'Have you been out on your own?'

'Yes.' Her blue eyes sparked. Anything wrong in that?'

'Plenty. It's asking for trouble to let a kid your age run round a game reserve as if it were a play park. Your father should have more sense. Or were you just taking advantage of his absence?'

'No, I wasn't! And I'm no kid.' Her heart was sinking more by the second. Were they going to have to put up with this substitute for the whole of the six weeks? She studied him from beneath her lashes, taking in the broad shoulders beneath the bush shirt, the general hardness of his tall, lean body, the tanned angular features and thick sweep of dark brown hair. He was what? Thirty-two? Thirty-three? Surely not old enough to have the kind of sweeping authority his tone suggested. And certainly nowhere near old enough to have the kind of experience both her father and Bruce Madden possessed.

She realized suddenly that he was looking right back at her with a glint of amusement in his eyes, and felt herself colour. Were her thoughts that obvious? She said swiftly, 'I suppose you've already met Ted Willis?'

'I haven't met anyone yet, apart from your two house servants,' he returned. 'But then I've only been here about an hour. Perhaps you can tell me where the devil everybody is.'

'Kimani Ngogi is out tracking down some poachers,' she said. 'He took four rangers with him, the rest are out on patrol. Ted must be around somewhere. He wouldn't leave the station unmanned.'

'I hope not.' The words were soft but meaningful. 'It strikes me that the whole set-up round here could do with looking into.'

Sara's chin lifted sharply. 'Do you think I might come in, now that you've finished your summing up?' she asked sarcastically. 'I'm hot and I'd like a drink.' She reached up and extracted the cigarette-case from Kiki's clutching paw, then put the monkey down on the veranda rail before moving on up the steps. 'I assume this is yours.'

He took it from her, mouth twitching a little at the corners. 'Thanks,' he said.

Sara stepped past him and went through into the shadowed living-room with its bare wooden floors and scattered skin rugs. With some deliberation she took bottles and glasses out of the cabinet, splashed some gin into her customary orange juice and took a long swallow before turning her head to ask coolly if he would like a drink.

He had followed her in, and now stood leaning his weight against the door-jamb with his hands in the pockets of his slacks. He shook his head, then asked unexpectedly, 'How old are you?'

'Nineteen,' she replied shortly, and the dark brows lifted again.

'Really? I thought about sixteen. Not that it makes any difference. You're still not equipped to be off the compound without adequate protection.'

She said caustically, 'I suppose you'd think differently if I were a boy!'

'I might.' He ran an eye over her, and grinned. 'Lived out here long?'

'Three years. Long enough,' she added, 'to learn the dos and don'ts and abide by them. I'm perfectly capable of taking care of myself, Mr. York.'

'As capable as you are at taking care of that gun you left outside in the car?'

Sara could have kicked herself as well as him. She had completely forgotten about the gun. Not that it would do any good to say that this was the first time she had done such a thing. He wouldn't believe her. She put down the glass. 'You took my mind off it. I'll fetch it in now.'

He was standing in the same position when she got back. He held out his hand for the Winchester and checked it over, smiled a little grimly when he found it unloaded but handed it back without comment.

'How good are you with that?' he asked.

'Fair.' She added steadily, 'Would you like me to

demonstrate?'

He shook his head. 'It won't be necessary.'

She stared at him. 'What does that mean exactly?'

'It means,' he returned equably, 'that you'll not be leaving the compound unless you have one of the men with you while I'm in charge here. If I'm going to have to accept responsibility for you while your father's away it's going to be on my terms.'

'Nobody is asking you to accept any responsibility for me at all,' she retorted with heat. 'You might be all sorts of a big noise where you've come from, Mr. York, but it doesn't mean a thing to me. I'm not employed by the Department, and I'll go where I please!'

He eyed her consideringly for a long moment before answering. 'Don't count on it. You might be queen bee round here in your estimation, but in my book you're just a spoiled brat who badly needs some discipline. Not that I lay the blame for that at your door. If you've been allowed to run wild for the last three years it's only to be expected.' He straightened his body away from the jamb. 'How about showing me my room while we're waiting for the missing Ted to put in an appearance?'

'Find it yourself!' she flung at him furiously, and stalked out of the door, almost barging into the man who was coming up the steps. 'Welcome to the Palace,' she greeted him. 'The Crown Prince just arrived!'

Ted Willis's leathery features took on a surprised expression, then his eyes went over her shoulder and the surprise turned to uncertainty. 'Are you the relief?' he asked of the man standing in the doorway. 'We were expecting Bruce Madden.'

'So I gathered.' The other's voice was dry. 'I'm Steve York. Madden couldn't make it. You must be Ted Willis.'

'That's me.' The older man was clearly nonplussed. 'Sorry I wasn't here to say hallo when you arrived. I was checking stores in the back shed. Can't always hear a car from there.'

'Apparently not.' There was a slight pause, then Steve York added smoothly, 'I think you were going to show me where I'll be sleeping, Miss MacDonald.'

Sara hesitated, looked at Ted, then turned slowly back to face the newcomer. There was a definite glint in the grey eyes regarding her steadily from the doorway. He had quite obviously heard what she had said to Ted. Well, so what? He had asked for it. And she certainly wasn't going to be intimidated by him.

'All right,' she said, 'I'll show you your room, Mr. York.'

'You won't need the gun.' His mouth was sardonic. 'Let Ted put it away for you.'

She handed it over without a word, then walked past him and through the living-room to the far door. There were five doors leading off the corridor beyond. Sara opened the second one on the right and stood back to give him access. 'This is normally my father's. It's bigger than the spare. I'm next door, Kimani is on the other side and Ted across from him. The bath-shed is out back.'

He took a glance round the somewhat sparse furnishings and nodded. 'It will do fine. What time do you usually eat?'

'Eightish.' It was just gone five-thirty. She added

coolly, 'I can arrange something to be going on with, if you like.'

'Complete with arsenic, I imagine.' He turned to look at her, paused a moment, then said evenly, 'Look, it's going to be a long six weeks if you're intending to keep this attitude up. I was no more thrilled to find you here than you were to see me instead of Madden, but as we're stuck with it we're both of us going to have to make the best of things. All I'm asking for is a little co-operation.'

Sara looked back at him stonily. 'Is that what you call it?'

His jaw tautened. 'All right, if that's the way you want it. Only I warn you, there's a limit to how much I'm prepared to take from little girls with an overrated sense of their own importance. While I'm in charge here you'll do as you're damn well told! Is that clear?'

'Crystal,' she retorted, and left the room trembling with anger. Hateful man! A regular despot! Give someone like that a little power and it went straight to their heads. Well, she'd be blowed if she was going to knuckle under. It was time somebody showed Mr. Steve York just where he got off!

Taking clean jeans and a shirt out of the limba-wood wardrobe in her own bedroom, she caught a glimpse of her face in the mirror, streaked with dust down both cheeks. She must have got that down by the river. Her hair was a mess too. All in all, it wasn't all that surprising that the man next door had taken her for a mere kid at first, although the memory of that comment still stung. She heard his door open again and his

15

footsteps going back along the corridor. He would be going to supervise the unloading of his car, she supposed. She hoped Ted wasn't available to help.

Out in the bath-shed she had a quick shower and got into the clean clothes, then slicked a brush over her damp hair and slung her soiled things into the basket outside. Tomorrow they would turn up clean and neatly pressed again on her bed. Maswi and Njorogi were the best house servants the station had known to date. Sara hoped they would stay, but doubted it. Because Kambala was so far removed from their home territory the pay was well above the usual rate, but that was small compensation for lack of communication with their own people. The obvious solution would be to try to persuade the Masai themselves to take over such tasks, only they didn't seem interested in the things which money could buy. Their wealth lay in their cattle which provided them with everything they needed. They were the most contented people she had ever known.

Ted was over by the water tank checking the level. Sara leaned against one of the supports to watch him, one leg drawn up under her like a crane. 'Did I use too much?'

His grin was tolerant. 'You always use too much. You can never get through to a female that showers are supposed to conserve the stuff. You should have seen the amount we were limited to on trek in the old days. A cupful for washing, if you were lucky!'

Sara laughed. 'So you keep telling me. In fact, if half of what you say is true it's a wonder the animals couldn't smell you coming a mile off!'

She was very fond of Ted Willis. He was actually only a few years older than her father, but a lifetime in the open had lined his features until they looked like a map of the Himalayas – his own description. In his prime he had been a hunter, and a good one. Then his eyesight had begun to deteriorate, and there had come a time when he could no longer compete with the other safari organizers in pinpointing game for his clients to shoot at. He had been here on Kambala when Sara had arrived, and had whiled away many an hour for her with his tales of the old days, although she strongly suspected that a great many of his anecdotes went back a good deal further than he did.

'Is Kimani back yet?' she asked.

Ted shook his head. 'He might have gone over to the Lodge.'

'You don't think they'll have found anything, then?'

'Doubt it. These lads are clever. Slip in over the boundary at night and out again before morning, and nothing to show they've been in apart from the carcases. The only way they stand much chance of being caught is if somebody finds the place where they've been lying up during the day and waits for them to come back in the morning.'

'And it's only the rhino horn they're going for?'

'It's all this particular lot are going for. They're well paid for what they get by the men outside organizing them, but it's those who don't take any risks who gain the real profit. Mind you, if somebody would get round to educating the folk who think the stuff's going to give 'em a boost the bottom would drop right out of the

17

market. It's been scientifically proved that there's nothing in this notion about powdered horn being an aphrodisiac. They'd get the same results from a dose of salts if they believed it!' He caught Sara's swiftly concealed grin and shook his grizzled head at her in mock reproof. 'You might laugh, girl, but it's true. Supply and demand, that's what it's all about. Cut out the last and there's no money in the first.'

'I believe you,' she said. 'I just thought the salts sounded a bit drastic.' She paused, glanced back at the house, said on a different note, 'What do you think of Dad's replacement?'

Ted lifted his shoulders. 'Remains to be seen. Not important, is it? He's only going to be here for six weeks.'

'I've a feeling it's going to seem more like six years,' she said gloomily. 'He's so darn full of himself. He even tried to tell me I couldn't go off the compound without a guardian.'

'Brave man.' Ted's voice was light. 'And what did you say?'

'What do you think? I've always . . .' She stopped, looked at him suspiciously. 'You don't agree with him?'

'I don't think it's a bad idea,' he admitted. 'It's something I've been telling Dave for the last couple of years. No matter how careful you are there's always something could happen. Supposing you got bitten by a snake?'

'There's serum in the car.'

'You might not be able to reach it in time. A mamba's poison only takes seconds to work through the

18

system. Okay, so nine times out of ten most things will get out of your way rather than attack, but you only have to come across that awkward customer once. Think you could stop a rhino with that three-seven-five you carry?'

'I'd never get near enough to precipitate a charge.' Sara kicked at a stone lying on the ground in front of her. 'I thought you'd be on my side.'

'I didn't know there were any sides to take. If this new chap says you're to stick with a partner then you'll have it to do. He's the boss till your father gets back. If you weren't prepared to accept that you should have gone with him.'

'I don't think he wanted me to go,' she said on a suddenly thoughtful note. 'At least, he didn't try very hard to persuade me. Do you think he could have been afraid that I might decide to stay in England?'

There was a brief pause before Ted answered. 'Could be,' he said at last. 'What you don't see you're not likely to realize you've missed. He'd hate to lose you.'

'There's no chance of that. He knows how I feel about things out here.'

'Now, yes. You haven't had much opportunity for comparisons this last few years, have you?'

Sara looked up quickly. 'What are you trying to say, Ted?'

'Nothing much. Just that there's going to come a time when you'll start wanting more than this place can offer, and he'll have to face it. He should have got married again. There's been more than one woman would have been glad to say yes to Dave Macdonald.'

'He never wanted to get married again.' She pushed herself away from the post, eyes bright. 'Dad's happy as he is. We both are.'

Ted eyed her shrewdly. 'I wonder. It might be the best thing that's happened to you two for years, being parted for a few weeks. Give you both time to realize that it's a daughter he's got, not a son.'

Sara stared at him disconcertedly. 'I thought you were supposed to be his friend.'

'I am. Doesn't mean I have to go about in blinkers. Dave's a grand chap, but where you're concerned he's as selfish as they come. He taught you to shoot like a boy, act like one, even think like one. I can't remember the last time I saw you wearing a dress.'

'Why should I? I'm more comfortable in pants. They . . .' She broke off abruptly. 'You don't know what you're talking about. I'm no different from any other girl my age!'

'No?' A smile creased his features. 'How about asking Steve York for his opinion on that score?'

She said loftily, 'I'm not in the least bit interested in his opinions on any score. And as you seem intent on pulling Dad's character to pieces when he's not here to defend himself, I'll leave you to it.'

She strolled over to the cookhouse with a coolness she was far from feeling, peered into the steamy interior to have a word with the African working there, then went back into the house and her own room. There, for the first time in years, she stood in front of the mirror and really studied her reflection, putting a hand to her short hair and flicking up the ends, running the tip of her tongue over lips which hadn't seen lipstick for heaven knew how long, straightening the collar of her shirt. Gradually there grew in her the suspicion that Ted might just be right. She did look more like a boy than a girl. She didn't know why that realization should bother her, yet it did a little. Not that it made any difference, she told herself firmly. She refused to change her habits simply to please Ted Willis – or anyone else for that matter. Trousers and short hair *were* more comfortable out here. She had found that out early on. And if her father didn't mind her looks why should anyone else?

Night came with its usual swiftness. Sara wandered through to the living-room at seven, and found it still empty. She browsed through a couple of magazines from the outdated pile on the rack for a few minutes, but found herself too restless to concentrate. She was glad when Kimani Ngogi came up the steps from the compound to join her.

'When did you get back?' she asked as the young Kenyan mixed himself a drink. 'I never heard the car.'

'About an hour ago,' he replied. 'We abandoned the search about four.'

'You found nothing then?'

'Only a couple of darts they'd dropped. They've either moved out of the district altogether, or they're lying low in the hope that we'll think just that.'

'Ted thinks they're coming in across the boundary each night.'

'I don't think so. Not this last time. The kill was too far in. No, I'd say that someone is slipping across with transport at night and taking the horn from them. We did see signs of a vehicle at one point, but it led to nothing. They could quite well have been made by that camping party who came in a week ago. They were in that sector for a couple of days.'

'So what happens now?'

'That's up to the new boss.' The aquiline features were impassive. 'I'd say that he'll go strictly by the book. He told me I should be concentrating on my own job, not chasing about doing someone else's.'

On the face of it, Sara supposed that Steve York was right. Kimani was here as a member of the Department's research staff, and as such his present duties were clearly laid down: to record the changing distributions of animal concentrations within the area. He had been on Mara for two months, and might be here another two. Certainly chasing poachers was not what he was paid to do.

'What's your opinion of him?' she asked.

'Why should I have one?' he returned equably. 'He's here to do a job of work like the rest of us. How he does it is his affair, and the Department's.'

'You can forget the Department. Bwana York runs his own little show.' She smiled with determined cheerfulness. 'I suppose it would be uncharitable to hope that he breaks his neck between now and dinner time.'

'Futile,' corrected the sardonic voice from the other doorway, and Sara jumped. 'Walls have thin ears.'

'And eavesdroppers rarely hear any good of themselves,' she came back on a creditably steady note. 'I hope you don't expect an apology.'

'From you it would be the last thing I'd expect.' He

moved into the room, nodded pleasantly to Kimani and helped himself to whisky. 'Cheers,' he said in Sara's direction.

She gave him a look meant to wither and turned her attention ostentatiously back to her magazine, trying her best to ignore the lean figure as he lowered himself to a chair close by. There was a moment when she thought he was going to say something else, then Ted came in and his attention became refocused. In the following half hour he proceeded to ply the other two men with questions regarding station procedure, quick intelligent questions designed to put him in the picture with the minimum of delay. Watching him covertly from over the top of the magazine, Sara could sense his dissatisfaction with some of the answers, and she bitterly resented the criticism of her father implicit in his attitude. A man of his kind would always think that his own methods had to be best, but it didn't necessarily follow. Her father had run this station for almost four years, and there had never been any complaints.

At eight Maswi brought in the fish rolls and curry, slapped them on the table and departed wearing a doleful expression. He and Njorogi were brothers, yet as different as chalk from cheese. Sara had a feeling that very soon now the former would talk the latter into going home. No one could stop them, of course, but it meant a long trek for someone to take them back to their home village the far side of Narok.

Seated in what was usually her father's place at the table, Steve York looked big, over-confident and almost aggressively masculine. Sara ate through the meal in silence, listening to the conversation going on around her without making any attempt to join in. Ted glanced at her quizzically once or twice but made no comment. For all the notice Steve York took of her she might not have been there at all. He was too interested in what Kimani had to tell him about his findings over the last two months, already involved in station affairs up to his neck.

'In the morning I'll have a go at picking up this trail you were following today,' he said to Kimani over coffee on the veranda. 'If you're right about them coming in across the boundary to pick up the stuff at night then those tracks might help to pinpoint the spot. Of course, it may turn out that they were made by those campers you were talking about, but at least it's a chance.' He glanced across to where Sara lounged in her chair with her feet slung up on the rail, added pleasantly, 'Is there any more coffee?'

She refrained from telling him to get it himself with an effort, and heaved herself to her feet to take his cup, meeting the grey gaze levelly. If he thought he was relegating her to her proper place in the scheme of things here he was mistaken. Come the morning he would find out how far his tactics went with her. She had already made her plans for the following day, and didn't intend to change them.

Both Kimani and Ted shook their heads when asked if they would also like another cup. She refilled Steve's and handed it back to him without a word, then dropped down the steps and strolled off into the darkness of the compound with an air of nonchalance.

The fawn was already bedded down in the shelter made for it in the far corner of the pen. It raised its tiny head when Sara approached and regarded her without fear, nostrils quivering. She stroked the soft nose and throat, thinking that she might soon start choosing a name for it. She never did that normally. It didn't do to become too attached to the young animals and birds she looked after; the wrench of parting was grim enough as it was.

The crickets were loud, the air full of familiar scents and smells. Sound carried for miles in these parts, each one separate and identifiable. She could hear splashings from the direction of the hippo pool above the rapid, the far-off barking of zebra out on the plain and, very much nearer, the persistent wailing of a solitary hyena. Sara recalled the sheer irrational terror of those first nights when she had lain awake trying to identify the different cries, calls, screams in her mind with something real and alive. Oddly enough the roar of the lion had always comforted her. She could recognize that, visualize the animal from which it had emerged. Only the unknown was frightening. There were still night noises she couldn't place, of course, but the fear had gone. These days it was silence she found unnerving.

As if in answer to her thoughts a pair of lions began roaring at each other across the river, and were immediately joined by another pair, further away but still distinct. The fawn jumped, its heart fluttering wildly beneath her soothing fingers. She talked to it quietly, and it grew calm again. When she left it was almost asleep, although the lions were still sounding off in chorus. Sara wondered if either pair belonged to the pride she had watched out on the plain a couple of days ago. There had been about twenty animals altogether, including half a dozen cubs of varying ages. It always fascinated her the way all the lionesses in a pride would feed any cub without regard to ownership or responsibility. Theirs was the true community spirit, achieved by instinct, not design.

She was standing with her back resting lightly against one of the corner posts still listening to the night when the sense of another presence impinged itself upon her consciousness. When she turned her head Steve York was lolling a few feet away in a similar pose watching her. Out here they were beyond the muted circle of radiance stretching out from the house, and in the darkness he seemed bigger than ever. An odd sensation swept over her, leaving her suddenly uneasy and on edge. Instinctively she sought refuge in attack.

'Is it necessary to keep a fatherly eye on me here in the compound too? Or did you have some other reason for following me?'

He didn't move. 'Such as?'

Sara pushed herself away from the post and stuck her hands in her pockets. 'How should I know? How long have you been watching me?'

'A couple of minutes.' He put a cigarette to his lips and flared a lighter, briefly illuminating the faint smile on his lips. 'I wanted to talk to you.'

She eyed him obliquely. 'About what?'

'You.' He paused, blew out a thin stream of smoke. 'I've got a sister your age staying with some friends in Nairobi. How would you like to go down there yourself for a couple of weeks? Jill would be glad of your company, and it would be a change for you.'

Her heart jerked. 'I don't need a change. If you're just looking for a way of getting me out of your hair, why not say so?'

'If that's all it was I'd hardly be so ready to park you on the Milsons,' was the dry reply. 'It seems to me that a change of scene would do you good.'

She said tautly, 'You've been talking to Ted.'

'A bit. The circumstances called for it.'

'They're not so special.'

'No?' He studied her across the three feet of moonlit space. 'When did you last wear a pretty dress, or grow your hair long, or listen to any conversation which wasn't exclusively male?'

'I don't just listen,' she said. 'I normally contribute. And my hair and clothes are suited to the kind of life I lead.'

'I know. That's the whole point. Stuck out here you're being denied an essential part of your growing-up. You need contact with others of your own age-group. Boys as well as girls.'

'With the eventual aim, I suppose, of finding myself a husband and settling down to a life of domestic bliss.'

His mouth pulled into a grin. 'There are worse things.'

'Are you married?'

'No, but it's different for a man.'

'You mean you're allowed to be individualistic and I'm not even supposed to want to be, don't you?'

'You haven't had much chance to know what you do want to be.' His gaze was speculative. 'You could be a very pretty girl, Sara, if you stopped playing the little tough. Don't you ever think about what you're missing?'

'At the moment I don't seem to be missing anything. I'm sure thousands would give their right arm to have Steve York take such an interest in their welfare. I don't want to go to Nairobi, and you can't make me.'

'I didn't say I could make you. It was just a thought.' His voice had gained an edge. 'But let's have one thing straight from the start. If you're going to stay here on the station you're going to have to learn to behave like a rational adult. You've been a tomboy long enough; it's time you started to listen to reason. I'm going to have enough on my plate without worrying myself silly over you!'

Fists clenched at her sides, Sara watched him stride purposefully away towards the house. Enough on his plate, had he? He hadn't even started yet!

# CHAPTER TWO

It was dawn when Sara awoke. She got out of bed swiftly and pulled on the jeans and shirt she had worn the previous night, put on a sweater over them and donned a pair of comfortable old riding boots into which she tucked the legs of her pants.

The sky was already a clear pale blue when she got outside, the tops of the trees showing golden against the slanting rays of the rising sun. Detail grew about her as she began the climb to the top of the bluff behind the house, the rock beneath her fingers taking on warmth and colour. Something moved in the undergrowth below; there was a glimpse of yellow-spotted fur, and then it was gone. Hyena, thought Sara, hitching the binocular case more firmly over her shoulder. They often came prowling round the compound like that, attracted by the smell of food. Once a pair of them had even dug their way in and tried to find a way into the store-hut. The tracks had been there the next morning to prove it, along with the damage.

She reached the narrow cleft which was her aim, and made the usual check for snakes before sitting down with her back to the rock. She often came up here in the mornings. It was such a superb spot from which to view the land she loved. Beyond the river with its forest-edged banks, the plains stretched limitlessly, broken only by termite mounds and the flat-topped acacia trees on which giraffe loved to feed. With the dawn mist dispersed and the heat haze not yet formed it seemed possible to see to the ends of the earth, every detail in between picked out with a sharpness which in itself made the scene almost unreal. The thousand feet of the Escarpment looked painted against the pale backdrop of the western sky, thirty miles away yet close enough to reach out and touch.

From here Sara could see the whole of the station compound. Ted came out of the house after a while and began giving Steve York's Land-Rover a check before breakfast. Several minutes later he was joined by Steve himself, and the two men stood talking together before going back indoors. Sara remembered the night before when he had followed her out into the compound, and felt her nerves quiver. He hadn't been here twenty-four hours yet, and already he was spoiling everything. If only Bruce Madden had come, or better still, if her father hadn't been forced to make this trip. She didn't like change, especially when it came in the shape of an autocrat like Steve York.

She turned away to scan the plains again for the last time before going down. There were zebra out there, and wildebeeste, and way over by the largest clump of trees within her immediate range, a group of giraffe browsing delicately among the upper branches. Suddenly they were on the move, cantering off with a haughty elegance which suggested reservation rather than fear.

Sara moved the glasses to find out what had spoofed them, saw a movement among the long grass to the right of the trees and sharpened the focus. Three Africans dressed in the brown togas and capes of the

Masai herdsman emerged slowly and cautiously into the open patch of burned, cropped grassland which stretched up to the next ridge, the sunlight glinting off the barrels of the guns all three held in their hands. They stopped and conferred for a moment, one lifting a hand towards the ridge as though indicating the way they must go. There seemed to be some argument, and then all three melted back into the thicket from which they had come.

They were going to work their way round the perimeter of the clearing, Sara surmised, instead of taking the risk of being caught out in the open by anyone who might conceivably come along. She got swiftly to her feet and pushed the field-glasses back into their case. They weren't Masai, of that she was certain. They were too small, and their skins not dark enough. She wondered if they knew how close they were to the station, and why they were on the move at such an hour. Not that the whys and wherefores mattered at the moment. There were more important things to think about.

The downward journey took her about a third of the time. Reaching the bottom, she set off through the low brush towards the compound at a trot. Steve was smoking a cigarette on the veranda. He watched her vault the fence and cross to the house expressionlessly, straightening away from the rail as she reached him to pinch out the remains of the cigarette between finger and thumb and toss it into the bin below.

'Where did you just come from?' he asked.

'Up there.' Sara waved a hand vaguely in the direction of the bluff. 'Can we leave the explanations till

later? I think I've seen the poachers – or *some* poachers, at any rate.'

He came instantly alert. 'Where?'

'I'll show you.' She was already moving towards the
corner of the house. 'We'll have to hurry or we'll lose
them.'

'You're staying here.' He shouted instructions in
Swahili to the two Africans out in the compound, then
threw a leg over the rail and jumped down in front of
her. 'Which direction? Quickly!'

Sara's chin jutted. 'You don't know the area like I
do. It would take too long. And I might point out that
the longer you argue about it the more chance they
have of getting away.'

The expression in his eyes boded ill for the not too
distant future, but the truth in her statement was too
apparent to be ignored. 'All right,' he clipped. 'Get in
the car.'

Sara walked across and got into the front passenger
seat, greeting the two rangers already seated in the
back with a cheerful *Jambo*. Steve slid in beside her
after pausing a moment to tell Ted where they were
going. He put the car into gear and turned in a wide
circle to take the track leading down to the river.

It took them a good ten minutes to reach the point
where Sara calculated she had seen the three Africans,
and another six or seven to round the ridge for which
she was certain they had been making. Beyond lay
savanna country, divided into rough fields by the
straight lines of the thicket hedges called *dongas*. Steve
stopped the car and stood up through the open roof to
survey the terrain through field-glasses, sweeping

round in a wide arc to cover every direction. Already the heat was rising fast, the distances shimmering and dancing. There were a thousand places where the Africans could be concealed if they'd heard the car. Sara doubted that they could have got very far beyond this. There hadn't been the time.

There was a movement in the near thickets, and a grey tank of a shape came lumbering slowly into the open, huge horned head lifted to sniff the wind. The rhinoceros knew there was something there, but was too short-sighted to make out just what. He moved closer, stood still and considered, then curiosity overcame caution and he came on at a slow trot. Without haste Steve dropped down again into the driving seat and veered off to the right. Looking back, Sara saw the rhino make a half-hearted effort to charge, then sink back to walking pace, its head going down to browse. They were so unpredictable. You never could tell just which way they were going to react. Stupid, her father always said. Incredibly stupid. Nevertheless a serious attack could reduce a vehicle like this one to a wreck in a very short time. She had seen an example of that herself.

They were in among the thorn scrub now, the murderous two-inch spikes scraping along the sides of the car and inflicting the same long, rusty-looking scratches as borne by the rhinoceros themselves on their armour-plated hides. There was no wind, nothing moving, just the noise of the engine and the odd whistling sound made by the thorns as they sprang back into position. If the poachers were hiding in here they certainly couldn't be very comfortable. They came out into an open patch again, jolting through tall, coarse grass which could have concealed a hundred men. Seventy yards away a couple of heads lifted sharply, scattering their attendant flocks of oxpeckers as the rhinoceros began to trot forward. This time it was the animal element which did the veering, turning off suddenly into a dense clump of thorn and disappearing from view.

Steve said abruptly, 'We might as well get back. There's nothing here.'

Sara looked at him quickly. 'I'm sure this is where they were heading. I saw one of them point towards the ridge.' She studied the lean, hard profile and knew a moment's pure rage. 'You don't believe me, do you? You think I made the whole thing up!'

'I'm not sure what I think,' was the grim reply. 'Try convincing me some more.'

Her eyes flashed. 'Go to blazes,' she said furiously. 'You can think what you like! It's the last time I ever . . .'

'Save it.' His voice was harsh.

The rangers were listening avidly to every word, although probably understanding only a few, and they were both smiling broadly. Sara bit her lip and subsided into her seat. She had forgotten the company.

They made the return journey in complete silence. Before the car came to a proper stop in front of the bungalow, Sara jumped out and made for the steps. She was half-way up them when Steve's hand closed about her upper arm like a vice, spinning her round to face him.

'You speak to me like that again in front of the men,'

34

he said roughly, 'and I'll give *you* something to think about. And that's a promise!'

Sara opened her mouth, caught his eye and closed it again abruptly. She gave him a look of sheer malevolence and went up the steps and along the veranda to the spot just around the corner where the breakfast table was laid. Ted and Kimani were already seated, and it was apparent from both their faces that they had heard what Steve had said to her. With a nonchalance she was a long way from feeling, she poured herself some coffee and seized a piece of toast, then moved away to the nearest chair and sat down in it, slinging both feet up on the rail. By the time Steve appeared she was munching away on the toast as if that were her only interest in life.

'No luck?' asked Ted as the other man took a seat.

'No.' The single negative discouraged further inquiry. 'Are you planning that aerial survey for today, did you say?' he asked Kimani, and receiving an affirmative, 'Then perhaps you'd take Sara along and drop her at the Lodge for the day. There was a party of English flying down when I left Nairobi yesterday morning.'

'I'd rather stay here, thanks,' Sara said expressionlessly.

There was a brief pause, then he said, 'Fair enough. See that you do.'

If he hadn't added that last she might just have decided to change her mind about her proposed plans, but the deliberation in his tone was a red rag to her spirit. She finished the toast and coffee without haste, sat for a few minutes longer listening idly to the conversation, then got to her feet and sauntered past the three men. Kiki swung down from an overhanging branch of the huge Candelabra Euphorbia which shaded the whole of this side of the house, landing on her shoulder to shrill protests into her ear. He hadn't had his breakfast yet. Sara took him round and into the living room and gave him a banana from the dish on the table, leaving him there to eat it while she went out again to see to the fawn.

She was in the pen when she heard the Land-Rover start up again. She didn't look up as it swept past and down the track to vanish among the trees.

Kimani left soon afterwards for the airstrip belonging to the Lodge, where a light plane was kept by the Department. He was an accomplished pilot with over a hundred flying hours to his credit. Sara had been up with him several times and enjoyed the experience. From the air he could pick out the animals he had marked among the various herds, and thus check upon movement in a way which was virtually impossible from the ground. She could, she supposed, have quite well gone with him again today. Kim never minded company providing they knew enough about his work to be a help and not a hindrance. For a brief moment she regretted that she hadn't thought of it sooner, but it was too late now.

Ted had one of the cars stripped down when she came out from the house with the Winchester in her hand. He wiped his hands on an oily rag as he watched her climb into the driving seat of the spare, a resigned look on his face.

'I'm going to the village,' Sara informed him. She

gave him a wide, bright smile. 'If I'm not back before sundown tell the Boss man I decided to go native.'

'It's your neck,' he returned, and grinned suddenly. 'Although I'd say it's probably the other end that's going to suffer most if he gets back before you do!'

'Hooey,' she said firmly, and started the engine before he could make any further comment.

She took the same route she had taken the previous day, cutting up from the river where she had watched the crocodile and over the ridge. Near where the steep rough rise began and the tall grass ended she saw a lioness and two cubs, the mother standing guard on a slightly higher piece of ground while her offspring tumbled in the grass below her feet. Sara slowed to get a better view, feeling safe enough at a distance of some fifty feet. The lioness ignored her, looking the other way with the same disdainful air adopted by any household tabby when not in the mood for confrontation, but Sara knew that should she put one foot to the ground that indifference would be a thing of the past inside of a second. Respecting the big cat's right to privacy, she drove on after only a moment or two, happy to have seen a family scene like that so close.

The herdsmen had long left the village with their herds by the time she got there, but the usual guards stood outside the entrance to the *boma*, tall, holding taller spears, motionless, like figures cast in copper bronze. The central *kraal* was crowded with people; two new huts were under construction and everyone available had been roped in to help. So far they only had the uprights erected on one, but the other was already plastered with dried dung on the inside walls

37

and was in the process of being roofed. They would both be ready for occupation before nightfall.

Sara was greeted from all sides, eagerly, as a friend. She had brought sweets for the children who gathered about her like bees round a honeypot, and she shared them out meticulously, placing one in each small palm held out to her and holding up her hands when they were gone to prove it. There was no pushing and pulling as one might expect to find in a similar crowd of European children, just a ring of beaming faces and moving jaws.

Mgari was seated outside his hut as always, his proud, aquiline head lifted to her approach. His *Jambo* befitted a headman, dignified and calm. She squatted at his side to talk to him for a moment or two in a mixture of Swahili and Masai, until he saw fit to summon his wives to meet her. She was privileged to have him take this much note of her, she knew. Magari's own womenfolk were more often than not ignored in public. Kept in their place, she supposed you could call it. It was strange to think that but for circumstances Kimani Ngogi might have lived in such a village as this, a warrior perhaps like those on guard at the entrance. He had stepped across time, learned the white man's language, received a university education and made a place for himself in the world outside. Whether he was luckier than these of his people who still lived the way they had lived for thousands of years was open to question. These people were totally unacquisitive, tuned to their surroundings, untroubled by modern-day complexities. In many ways they were to be envied.

Lawino eventually brought out her latest-born child to show. It was a boy, perhaps a week old, his little bronze body already decked out with brightly coloured beads and ornaments made from cowrie shells. When he started to cry she put him to her breast, squatting on the ground at Sara's side and smiling shyly. She was beautiful, her features finely chiselled and serene, her shaven head perfect in shape. Round her neck she wore rings of coloured beads like those on her child, and her arms were heavily festooned with bracelets. Mgari regarded her with tolerance, even indulgence. She was obviously his favourite.

It was past midday before Sara eventually stirred herself to leave. A whole group of villagers accompanied her regretfully to the car, speeding her on her way with the soft *sere sere* of their farewell, and standing there smiling and waving until she was out of sight. She felt happy and content herself. She always did after a visit to the Masai *boma*. Coming down to the spot where she had seen the lioness and her cubs, she decided to cut off from the track across the plain and approach the station via the shallow neck of river half a mile beyond. She was glad she had remembered to bring a hat for once. Even the Rover's canvas roof failed to give full protection from the fierce weight of the sun at this hour.

The great herd of wildebeeste she had spotted from the bluff had moved only a matter of a mile or so. She passed within twenty feet of them slowly, but the sentry animals on the edge of the herd did no more than keep an eye on her between mouthfuls. She had left them and was within three miles of home when her offside front wheel found the deep hole left by some long-gone burrower, and it was only sheer luck which kept her from overturning the vehicle. Recovering from her momentary fright, she tried to back the car out, and listened to the resulting row with her heart sinking slowly into her shoes. From the crazy angle of the front wheel down there the bearing had certainly gone, but that couldn't be causing all the noise. With a superficial knowledge gained from watching Ted at work at various times, she could think of only one thing it might be – the front wheel drive shaft. Which meant that she was well and truly stuck.

How long she just sat there contemplating she had no real idea. There was an immense silence over the plains, broken only by the flute-like piping of a pair of bou-bou shrike floating up from the direction of the river. At this time of the day most of the animals were resting in the shade of tree and bush, waiting for the cool of the evening before exerting any further energy. Sara felt totally alone and helpless. In her two years of driving this was the first time anything like this had ever happened to her, and it had to be now of all times! She didn't even want to think about what Steve York was going to say when he found out what she'd done.

Eventually she galvanized herself into action. It was no use mulling over the 'if onlys' in her mind. She would have to contact Ted on the SSB and get him to come out and tow her in – always providing he'd got the other car put to rights again. She switched on the radio and put out the station call sign, hoping that somebody was near enough to the set to hear it. When the acknowledgment came through, however, it wasn't the station at all but Steve York picking up the call from the other car somewhere out in the bush.

'Where are you?' he demanded without preamble.

Sara took a deep breath before launching into her answer. She had to get it over some time, and it might as well be sooner as later. 'I'm three miles east of the Station with a front wheel in a hole,' she said clearly and succinctly. 'It sounds as if the drive shaft might have gone.'

There was the briefest of pauses. 'Are you hurt?'

'No.'

'Then stay put and wait. We're about fifteen miles away. Should be there in about forty minutes. Keep contact open, and *don't* get out of the car. Do you hear me?'

She could hardly fail to hear him when he barked like that, but for once she held the retort. 'I won't. Wouldn't it be quicker to get Ted to come out?'

The reply was not encouraging. 'Ted's turn will come. Over and out.'

The minutes dragged endlessly by. Where her back rested against the seat the whole of Sara's shirt was soaked with perspiration, and she could feel it trickling down the back of her neck from her scalp. Without the breeze created by movement the car was an oven at this hour, a torture chamber. Sara longed for the cool shade of the nearest clump of trees, but didn't fancy sharing it with a possible pride of lions or even a lone cheetah. Only an idiot would take a risk like that for the sake of mere comfort. Steve didn't come on the radio again, so she assumed he was on his way. She wished he would hurry up. Whatever he had to say when he did get here it was preferable to this interminable waiting.

She saw the Land-Rover when it was still a couple of miles off, bumping over the rough ground at no more than the recommended twenty miles an hour. Steve York went by the book all right. He probably knew it by heart! She waited until the other vehicle was mere yards away before sliding stiffly from her seat to stand up and stretch in the grass.

Steve drew to a stop and got out, gave her one brief cold glance and went round to the front end to have a look underneath. When he straightened things began to happen quickly. A rope was procured from the back of his own car by one of the rangers and attached to the front end of the other, which was then drawn from the hole. Being a four-wheeled drive vehicle the car was still moveable providing it was driven with care and concentration at a low speed. The two Africans were detailed to bring it in together, one walking in front to pick out the most level route. Then and then only did Steve finally turn his attention to Sara, jerking a thumb over his shoulder in the direction of his own car.

'Get in.'

Sara got. It was either that, she felt, or be put. It didn't take any special perceptive powers to judge his mood – he was blazing. She sat silently at his side as they jolted homeward for the second time that day, and had to admit to a certain growing apprehension concerning what was going to happen when they got there. He wouldn't touch her, she told herself. He wouldn't dare. Her father would certainly have something to say about it if he even tried! But her father was thousands of miles away in England by now, and anything he might say was six weeks away. She was on her own.

Ted was still working on the stripped-down car when they got in. He straightened from an inspection of the engine casing as they came up the track, surprise followed by disconcertion chasing across his face.

'What happened?' he asked.

'Enough. I hope we've got some spares in stock.' Steve's tone was clipped. 'I'm going to want words with you after I've got through with the Jungle Princess here.' His hand was on her arm, his fingers digging painfully into her flesh. 'You're surely to God capable of keeping an eye on a slip of a girl!'

He didn't wait for an answer, but shoved Sara ahead of him up the steps and into the house, put her into a chair and closed the door, then stood with his back to it looking at her with unnerving calculation.

'If you were a couple of years younger I'd whale the daylights out of you,' he said. 'In fact, I'm strongly tempted to do it anyway!'

'It was an accident,' she said at last. 'It could have happened to anyone.'

'It could,' he agreed. 'But it wouldn't have happened to you if you'd been here on the station.' He stuck his hands in his pockets as if afraid of what he might do with them otherwise. 'The trouble with you, my girl, is that you don't give a damn for anything outside of your own interests. You're spoiled rotten, and about as pigheaded as they come! You strut around like a young peacock, so full of your own importance you can't even see the kind of brat you're

43

making yourself look. If you really felt you had to leave the station today you could quite easily have taken one of the boys with you, but that would have been too much like giving in, wouldn't it? And Sara Macdonald never does anything which might smack of compulsion!' He paused to draw breath, eyed her hardily, added harshly, 'It's high time you had a few home truths. I spoke last night about sending you down to Nairobi to spend a few weeks with my sister, only I doubt very much that you could be relied on to behave as a guest might normally be expected to. Your father has one hell of a lot to answer for!' He turned then and opened the door, added over his shoulder, 'I'll leave you to brood on it. Just stay away from me for the rest of the day if you know what's good for you.'

Sara sat huddled numbly in her chair as the door banged behind him. She hadn't cried for years, but she felt very close to it now. Was that how everyone saw her – an empty-headed little popinjay without a single redeeming feature? Even thinking about the caustic, cutting comments made her wince. Steve York had known her less than twenty-four hours, and already he despised her. It hurt to realize that. It hurt badly. Yet what had she expected? She had deliberately set out to show him up, and in front of the men he was supposed to be in charge of for the next few weeks. The Africans respected authority; how would they feel now about a man who allowed a female to get away with the kind of flagrant defiance of it that she had displayed today? If Steve had thought about that – and he would have – he could have made certain of restoring that authority by dressing her down right out there on the plains where they could hear and appreciate. But he hadn't, even though he'd obviously wanted to. He'd granted her the privacy of a closed room before letting fly. She felt small and ashamed. She hadn't given the man a chance from the moment he had arrived.

Ted was sitting on the steps smoking a cigarette when Sara finally recovered her composure enough to feel up to facing the world again. He looked at her, gave his head a little shake and patted the space beside him. 'A bit like being run over with a steamroller, isn't it?'

'Did you hear?' she asked, low-toned.

'Most of it. Couldn't help it.' He shook his head again, wry humour touching his mouth. 'I got my share of it too for letting you take the car in the first place. He's not short of a word or two, that chap!'

'Sorry, Ted,' she murmured, and meant it. She hesitated before adding tentatively, 'Am I really as bad as all that? I mean all those things he said.'

'He had a few points,' he acknowledged at length. 'But generally speaking I'd say he went a bit far.' His smile was familiar, affectionate and comforting. 'There's more to you than meets the eye, young Sara. You just need the rough edges rubbing off, that's all — though not necessarily with a rasp.'

She curved an arm about the corner post, resting her cheek against the planed and sanded wood. She didn't know quite how she felt at the moment. It was like having a hollow inside her filled with a question mark. In all of her nineteen years of life she had never been called upon to stop and take a look at herself. Steve had been right about one thing, she didn't think she only reacted. And to him she had reacted violently. Why, she wasn't at all sure even now.

'Did he happen to mention anything about the poachers?' she asked after a while.

'Only that they'd lost the trail before your call came through. He was on his way back.' He gave her a sideways glance. 'Did you really spot that bunch this morning?'

She nodded. 'You don't think they could possibly be the same?'

'Doubtful. Unless they moved like greased lightning. What I can't understand is why they were taking a chance on being seen in broad daylight like that. They must have known the station was somewhere in the vicinity.'

'I think they might have been looking for a suitable place to hide up for the day.' Sara was looking into the middle distance, eyes reflective. 'I'm sure they weren't out on the savanna or we'd have seen some sign, yet they were definitely heading in that direction.' Her head came up suddenly. 'Ted, I've had an idea. You remember last year when I told you I'd seen a leopard up by the ridge and both you and Dad said it was probably a serval cat?'

He looked at her questioningly. 'Yes, why?'

'Well, this spring I came across what I think might have been its lair. There's a small cave on the far side right along towards the end. It's covered by thorn and takes some finding, but it's just possible that they did find it this morning. If they were in there when we went through it would explain why they seem to have disappeared without trace, wouldn't it?'

'Could be.' Ted didn't sound very convinced. 'Did you mention it this morning?'

'I've only just remembered about it.' The silence stretched out. Eventually, with reluctance, she said, 'I suppose I ought to mention it now while there's a chance of checking on it. Even if the three of them are there they'll leave it tonight as soon as it's safe to move. What do you think?'

'I think you're probably right,' he said after a moment, and she gave a small sigh.

'That's what I was afraid you'd say.' She let go of the post. 'Now I know what Daniel must have felt like. Give me a decent burial, won't you?'

Ted was grinning. 'You'll cope. You're bouncing back already. He went round the back.'

Steve was talking with a small group of the rangers when she rounded the corner of the house. He watched her approach without any visible alteration in his expression or pause in what he was saying, finishing off as she reached the group with a crisp *Ngoja kidogo* (wait awhile) to regard her with inquiringly lifted brows.

'Can I talk to you a moment?' she said, paused, and tagged on impishly, 'Please.'

His lips twitched, and were hastily controlled. 'About what?'

'The poachers.' She saw his jaw tense again, added quickly, 'No, really. I'm not trying to be funny or anything.'

He studied her for a long moment before he inclined his head. 'All right, I'll buy it. But make it snappy.'

Sara did. In as few words as possible she told him what she had suggested to Ted, and was rewarded by

47

the keen look which appeared in his eyes.

'You say this cave is on the far side of the ridge,' he said. 'How far along? What landmarks can we look for?'

She had thought about that. 'There's a dead tree almost directly in line with the entrance, about a quarter of a mile south of where we stopped this morning. If they hear you coming and make a break for it you'll still spot them. The nearest *donga* is several hundred yards away.'

'*If* they're there.' It was obvious from his tone that he still didn't wholly trust her to be telling the truth. He gave instructions to two of the rangers, who went off to fetch guns, then turned back to her. 'And you . . .'

'I know,' she said evenly, 'I'm to stay put. Don't worry, I'm suitably impressed.'

Steve grinned suddenly. 'So am I. Give Ted a break too, will you?' He put out a hand and maddeningly ruffled her hair in passing.

They were gone an hour. Sara was out front with Ted, who was still working on the first of the out-of-commission vehicles, when she heard the car returning. She waited eagerly for it to appear out of the trees, and counted only the same three passengers with a sense of deflation. She had been so sure that she was right about the cave. Now Steve would never believe her.

He stopped to say a few words to the men after he had got out of the car, before coming across to where she waited on the veranda, pushing his hat to the back of his head as he looked up at her. 'Seems you were right about the cave,' he said. 'They'd definitely been there, but they must have lit out again as soon as we left this morning.' His smile had a wry tilt. 'A pity you didn't remember about the cave then.'

'Yes.' She could think of nothing to add to that.

Ted said, 'I gather they didn't leave much of a trail.'

'None at all that we could spot. They'd be good and scared, and careful. They could be holed up anywhere by now.'

'Think they'll risk another kill in the area?'

'I'd say it was likely. By nightfall they'll have recovered their nerve enough to try it at least.' Steve slapped automatically at a fly crawling over his neck. 'I'll take some of the boys out after dinner and cruise round for a bit. If we don't actually catch them in the act we'll probably scare them off again for the time being.' His glance went to the car which had limped in some fifteen minutes previously. 'How long before you get around to fixing that?'

Ted shrugged. 'Morning. Too late to start to-night.'

'Right. If nothing else crops up I'll lend you a hand. How about a drink?'

'Wouldn't say no. I'm just about finished here.'

'I'll fetch them out to the veranda.' Steve came on up the steps and past where Sara stood to disappear indoors. She could hear the clinking of glasses, then the splash of a soda-syphon. When he came out again he was minus his hat and carrying a tray holding three glasses. He put it down on the table, picked up one of the glasses and held it out to Sara with a slight upward tilt of his lips. 'Orange juice with a splash of gin. Okay?'

She took it from him with an odd feeling of breathlessness, and had to make an effort to keep her voice light. 'Am I to be allowed to join the grown-ups, then?'

'Whilever you can keep the performance up.' He sat down, took a long swallow from his own glass and eyed her thoughtfully. 'I wouldn't mind knowing what's going on behind that doe-eyed innocence at the moment.'

Sara swirled the liquid in her glass. 'I thought you already had me all weighed up, Mr. York.'

'Ouch,' he said softly. 'Okay, so I got a bit rough on you. You've got to admit I had some reason.'

'I never said you didn't.' She thought of what Ted had said, and her eyes lit with sudden devilment. 'Only you have to realize that there's more than one bite in an apple.'

He laughed, his regard taking on a new slant. 'Unpredictable, aren't you, young Sara!'

'Just misunderstood,' she retorted. 'And don't patronize. I'm not that young.'

'Just enough to make me feel distinctly jaded.' His mouth curved again at her swift appraising glance, this time with a hint of irony. 'It isn't just a matter of years. Some day you might know what I'm talking about.'

'You mean when I've done all those things I'm missing out on now? Perhaps I'm not missing so much after all.' She turned her head to give Ted an innocent smile. 'Mr. York feels jaded, Ted. How do you feel?'

'Good enough for the next ten minutes or so,' was the grinning reply. He lifted his glass to them both. 'Cheers.'

Steve said lazily, 'One more of those Misters, and I'll cut your gin ration. What time does Kimani usually get back?'

'Just before dark.' She waited a brief moment before tagging on, 'Are you planning to ask him to go with you tonight?'

'No.'

'Oh,' she said.

'Neither,' he added in the same tone, 'am I planning on asking anyone else.'

Sara grimaced at her orange juice. 'Don't you ever let up?'

'Not when it might be taken for a sign of weakening. Habit dies hard. I'm suspicious by nature.'

'You're telling me!' She drained her glass and set it down. 'I'll do my best to conform to regulations. Permission to leave?'

His eyes were twinkling. 'Don't get too cocky with it. I'm going to be around some time yet.'

And that statement, thought Sara strolling into the house, was suddenly far less dismaying than it might have been a few short hours ago. There were ways of handling even a man like Steve York if one went about it with care.

The evening seemed unusually long after Steve had left to continue his search. Sara spent most of it out on the veranda thinking about the men out here on the plains, and wishing she were involved in the chase. It wouldn't have occurred to her father to even suggest her staying behind, she realized. But then he knew her a great deal better than Steve.

51

She wondered how he was making out in England. If Uncle Geoffrey had only left a will the whole matter could probably have been compressed into a few days. But he hadn't, and although her father was his only known living relative it appeared that the estate must go to probate, which meant that her father had to be there to sign legal documents at various stages. What he was going to find to do with himself for a whole six weeks, she couldn't begin to imagine, although he had mentioned something about looking up some old acquaintances.

She stirred restlessly, glancing across to where Kimani Ngogi sat writing a letter at the rickety wicker table. His parents lived down in Mombasa and he didn't see them very often, but he never missed a weekly letter.

'Do you have a girl-friend, Kim?' she asked suddenly, àpropos of nothing. 'A special one, I mean.'

He looked up smilingly. 'No,' he admitted. 'I never seem to have had the time.'

'But you're twenty-eight now,' she persisted. 'Surely you don't want to go on as you are all your life? You must have thought about it.'

'From time to time. Not with any great urgency. I was under the impression that I still had plenty of time.' His regard was quizzical. 'Why this sudden desire to see me tied down?'

Sara wasn't at all sure what had prompted the questioning herself. She grimaced at him. 'Why do men always talk about marriage like that?'

Kimani grinned. 'It's a habit I picked up in England. Perhaps it all stems from being limited to one wife. Take Mgari, for instance. He has three to fetch and carry for him. Maybe I missed out, being a third generation city-dweller. There's a lot to be said for the old ways.'

'You've said that before. Do you really regret not having had the chance to choose for yourself?'

'I did have the choice. There was nothing to stop me from reverting to the way of life of my forebears if I'd wanted it.' He shrugged. 'Let's face it, I could no more live in a mud hut than you could, no matter how strong the tie. I've been educated to a different cultural background, taught to need more than any *boma* could offer. There's a hundred years between Mgari and me, and no way of bridging the gap. You can stay as you are or you can move forward, but you can't go back.'

There was something in that latter statement which made her feel vaguely disturbed. She said slowly, 'I went out to the *boma* today.'

'Yes, I heard.' There was a slight pause before Kimani added evenly, 'I have to agree with Steve that you shouldn't have gone there alone at any time.'

'Why?' she demanded in some annoyance.

'Because they're simply not used to seeing white women wandering about on their own. The parties which drop in on them from time to time always have men in charge, which in their eyes is as it should be. Mgari grants you privileges he would extend to none of the women of his own race because he recognizes the essential differences between you, but he also realizes that this very indulgence disturbs the pattern of centuries in a way which can only be bad for the tribe in the long run.'

Sara was quiet for a long moment. 'I never thought of it like that before,' she admitted at last on a rueful note. 'In fact, I'm beginning to think that I never thought about *anything* much before.' She hoisted herself to her feet. 'I'm for bed to mull it all over. See you at breakfast.'

Perhaps she had been subconsciously listening, or maybe it was some prior noise which had brought her to the edge of sleep, but whatever the reason she came instantly and completely awake when the car came rumbling along the track from the river. The fingers of her watch stood at three-fifteen, and the night outside was as black as pitch. Rain hammered on the roof, washing down over the window in a constant stream to gurgle its way down through the cracks in the veranda planking and sink into the parched earth below. There was no wind, just the rushing water, and the creak of the front steps as feet mounted them.

Sara got swiftly out of bed and went to the door, standing there waiting. The clink of bottle and glass drew her forward and into the living-room doorway, where she paused a little uncertainly. Steve had obviously sloughed his coat and boots outside on the porch, but his trousers were soaked to the knee. In the light from the single lamp he looked tired and drawn, and he needed a shave. He half turned as he took the glass from his lips, saw her standing there in the doorway and leaned his weight against the cabinet at his back to survey her with faintly lifted brows.

'You should have something on your feet,' he said.

Sara glanced down at her cotton pyjamas and bare toes and felt the warmth touch her cheeks. It hadn't occurred to her to put anything else on. She had simply given way to impulse. 'How did it go?' she asked.

'Better than I hoped. We got two of them. The other got away, but I doubt that he'll present much of a problem on his own. Had to lose a rhino to do it, though.'

'Congratulations,' Sara said insincerely. 'Where are they now?'

'Being held at the Lodge until morning, when arrangements can be made to get them both down to Nairobi to stand charges.'

'So it's all over.'

'This time. They weren't the first, they certainly won't be the last.' He took another pull at the whisky, added grimly, 'It's the men behind them that I'd really like to get a line on. When this lot fail to turn up with the goods they'll simply recruit some other labour force.'

'Mightn't the two you've captured give them away?'

'It's doubtful that they know anything beyond the fact that if they turn up at an agreed place with an agreed bag they'll get paid so much *pesa.* The only real hope is the dart guns they were supplied with, although I'd say that tracing them is going to prove difficult.' He lifted broad shoulders. 'That's up to the authorities. Isn't it time you were getting back to bed?'

'I'll go when you go', she said without thinking, and saw the quick grin lift the corners of his mouth.

'A couple more years and that kind of statement could get you into trouble. If you feel like keeping me company come on in and take a pew. I wanted to talk to you anyway, and it might as well be now as in the morning.'

Sara sank into the nearest chair and eyed him somewhat warily. 'Talk to me about what?'

'If you can keep your hackles down for five minutes I'll tell you.' He studied her. 'I've been thinking about that suggestion I made for you to go and stay with Jill in Nairobi.'

'I'm not . . .' She caught herself up, amended her reply. 'I don't want to go to Nairobi.'

'I know you don't.' He was smiling a little. 'Are you going to let me finish?' He took her silence for agreement, and went on smoothly, 'The point is that I was planning to spend a few weeks with Jill for the first time in a couple of years when this job turned up, and there won't be another chance for some time to come. How do you feel about having her up here for a spell? She's never been to the highlands before, so it would be quite an experience for her to take back home to Mombasa at the end of the season.'

Sara's reactions were mixed. She was curious about Steve York's young sister, she had to admit, but she wasn't at all sure that she would welcome the company of a girl of her own age who'd spent the last three years in such a totally different background. If Jill was anything like her brother they'd probably be daggers drawn inside the first hour.

'Why are you asking me?' she murmured. 'You've a perfect right to bring anyone you like out here while you're the boss.'

He raised his eyes heavenward. 'You know, you'd try the patience of a saint! I'm asking you because I don't want trouble later on. Jill can stand up for herself all right, but she'd prefer not to have to. What I want to know is would you be prepared to welcome her without bringing out the beads and rattles?'

'Can't I even mutter a few incantations?'

'I've muttered more than a few since I got here.' He sounded distinctly exasperated. 'Just make up your mind which way you're going to blow and stick to it, will you?'

'Sorry.' She put on a penitent expression. 'I'll welcome your sister with open arms, if that's what you want. Does your family live in England?'

'There isn't any family. Just Jill and me.' He put the glass down, straightened away from the cabinet. 'I'll start making arrangements in the morning. She could come through on next week's supply plane.' His hand went down to ease the wet material away from his calves. 'If I don't get out of these soon they'll be drying on me. Come on, I'll see you safely tucked away first.'

Sara came abruptly to her feet. 'I'm past being tucked in, thanks.'

'Sure.' He sounded amused. 'In a manner of speaking, you're a big girl now. But so far as I'm concerned you're still a babe, so you can forget any doubts you might be getting about me in that direction. I like my women over twenty-five, and willing.'

'And preferably married too, I'll bet,' she flashed, stung. 'Single ones might get too many ideas!'

'You might have a point there. Not behind the door altogether, are you, poppet?' He grinned as her eyes blazed. 'Go on, scoot, while I'm still in a good mood.'

Sara went, shutting both doors behind her as loudly as she dared, half hoping that he would come after her to find the bolt already shot on hers. Poppet indeed!

# CHAPTER THREE

THERE was no further mention of Jill York's impending visit over the following few days. Steve was out on patrol soon after breakfast, not returning until late into the afternoon. Used to the freedom she had enjoyed prior to her father's departure, Sara found the restrictions placed upon her movements irksome to a degree, particularly when Ted refused to give her the keys to the gun rack.

'Sorry,' he said blandly. 'The boss said as you'd be having company on all your jaunts you wouldn't need it for the present.'

'I've never *needed* it yet,' she returned crossly. 'I'm just used to having it with me. I'll bet you wouldn't get him moving very far without a gun to hand.'

'No, well, it's a bit different, isn't it?' was the unmoved reply. 'I'm not risking another chewing out like that last one. If you want to argue the point you do it with Steve.'

'All right, I will,' she said. She wouldn't, and she knew that Ted knew she wouldn't. Arguing any point with Steve was totally futile where she was concerned.

She spent the whole of one day with Kimani looking for a certain herd of elephant he had spotted from the air, and on the next had one of the rangers run her out to the Lodge to bathe in the swimming-pool. She had the place almost to herself for the morning, the present

59

parties of tourists all being out with their guides on the plains. Towards lunchtime they began to filter back for the midday lull.

Sitting on the pool side with her feet dangling in the tepid water, Sara watched the movement between restaurant and bar and wondered if even one of those laughing, chattering people had gained anything special from their visit to the wilds of Africa. To most, a reserve was nothing more than a glorified zoo, except that here the human element occupied the cages while the animals roamed free. By this time next week or next month they'd all be back in their homelands, eagerly telling the tale of how they'd seen lion and elephant and rhinoceros in their natural habitat, proudly showing the photographs snapped from the windows of a slowly moving car as the guide angled for the best position. For one or two, perhaps, would come the fleeting memory of nights thick with sound and sunrises such as they would see nowhere else in the world, of the sheer fantasy of a herd of impala stretched in full flight, or the majesty of a single lion silhouetted against the evening sky, but they would be impressions they couldn't pass on because they wouldn't know how. No words could ever be enough.

Sara was on the verge of making a move into the shade herself when the young man who had come out from the restaurant area detached himself from the family group he was with to stroll across the grass to where she sat. As he approached closer, she saw that he was probably only a year or so older than she was herself though with an air of confidence which at a distance had led her to think him in his mid-twenties at least. He was smiling in a friendly fashion, hands thrust casually into the pockets of his shorts, fair hair lifting slightly in the light breeze which had sprung up.

'Say, you're new, aren't you?' he said. 'Get in this morning?'

Sara shook her head. 'I live here.'

'Here?' His good-looking young face registered surprise. 'At the Lodge?'

'Well, no. We're about twenty miles away.' She wrapped her arms about her knees. 'My father is Warden of Kambala Station.'

'Oh?' Interest replaced the surprise, and he sank to a seat on the grass beside her. 'Hey, that must be really something! Imagine actually living right out here! You must be a real adventurous type. I'm Travis Willard from Detroit.'

'Sara Macdonald. I've never met anyone from Detroit before,' she added, unable to think of anything else to say on the spur of the moment.

'Well, it's nothing like this, I can tell you – although the jungle bit still applies. We live sixteen floors up in an apartment block. On a clear day you can almost see the street.'

'We?'

'The family. Mother, father and younger brother. This trip was supposed to be my nineteenth birthday present, but we decided to wait another year and make it all together.'

Sara said, 'And has it been worth waiting for?'

'Sure has. Wouldn't have missed it.' He sounded genuinely enthusiastic. 'We've been to Aberdare and Amboseli, Nairobi and now this. I'm not looking forward to setting off for home the day after tomorrow, I can tell you.'

'You've certainly got around,' commented Sara. 'How long have you had?'

'A month. I've taken reels and reels of ciné film, so at least I'll have something to remember it all by.' He looked over his shoulder to where his family had settled themselves down on loungers along the shaded terrace. 'Say, why don't you come over and meet the folks? They'd be tickled pink to know you.'

She glanced down at herself uncertainly. 'Shouldn't I get changed first?'

'I don't see why.' His glance was frankly admiring. 'You look fine. I wish I could get a tan like that, but just catch and burn, so I have to watch it.'

'Then you'd better get into the shade,' she said, smiling at him. 'And I'd like to meet your family very much.'

The rest of the Willards proved to be as warmly friendly as the elder son, and soon made Sara feel at home in their midst. Travis's younger brother was aged about ten and was introduced simply as Chipper. He eyed Sara with suddenly awakened interest when Travis told them that she lived on the Reserve itself, freckling face lighting up.

'Can you ride an elephant?' he demanded without preamble.

Sara smiled and shook her head regretfully. 'I'm afraid not.'

'Well, have you got a pet lion, then?'

Again she had to acknowledge failure, and he began to look scornful. 'Gee whizz, you must have somethin'!

You can't . . .'

'Chipper!' warned his mother in a voice long accustomed to warding off embarrassing observations from her son. She glanced apologetically at Sara. 'He's been watching too many of those old Tarzan films on television. I think he expected to find everyone round here swinging from the trees.'

He wasn't alone in that, thought Sara, recalling some of the stories related by the guides after taking certain parties out for a day's sightseeing. According to them, some of the folk who came on these safari trips wouldn't have been at all surprised to see Tarzan himself come swinging through the trees!

'I do have a monkey,' she offered, wondering if that could possibly constitute an adequate substitute for a lion. Apparently it did have some merit, for Chipper's face regained its shine.

'What kind? A chimp?'

'No, it's a Sykes.'

His broad forehead wrinkled. 'I've never heard of one of those.'

'Oh, you've probably seen them in the zoo. It's sometimes called the Blue monkey, or *Kima* in Swahili.'

'Can you speak Swahili?'

Mr. Willard raised his eyes to heaven. 'Quiztime again! You've asked more questions than an encyclopedia could answer this last four weeks!'

'I don't mind,' Sara said quickly. 'I can speak enough to get by on,' she added to Chipper. 'There's a young fawn back at the Station, too – a dik-dik. That's about the smallest in the world.'

'Gosh!' The boy's eyes were round. 'Can I see it – and the monkey?'

'Chipper, how many times do I have to tell you about begging for invitations like that?' broke in his mother hastily. 'Of course you can't.'

Sara watched the glow start to die, and gave herself no time to consider. 'Oh, he can if he wants to. Why don't you all come over in the morning? You could easily get your guide to run you across.'

'Gosh,' said Chipper again. 'Can we really? Gosh, wait till I tell the kids at school about this! A real game station!'

'Are you sure it will be all right?' asked his father doubtfully. 'Won't your father mind?'

'My father isn't here at the moment,' she returned, already half regretting the impulse but seeing no fair way out of it. 'And of course it will be all right. If you like heights, Chipper, I can take you to a place where you'll be able to see all kinds of animals.'

'Hey,' chimed in Travis in mock indignation, 'what about me?'

'You too, if you want.' She smiled at him, pushing back a lock of hair which had fallen across her forehead, then felt the smile fasten itself on to her face as her gaze travelled over her shoulder and fell upon the man coming along the terrace towards their little group.

Steve came to a stop at the outer edge of the circle of chairs, tall and brown in the bush shirt and shorts, his hat as always pushed to the back of his head. He swept a provoking scrutiny over her scantily-clad form, said pleasantly:

'I thought you might be ready to go back, but there's no rush if you want to wait for Temu to fetch you.' The smile he directed at Mrs. Willard was easy and casual. 'Nice of you to take her under your wing for a bit. There isn't much company for a young girl out at Kambala.'

Sara clamped her teeth around the too ready retort. This wasn't the time to be getting his back up. She murmured introductions, explained Steve's position in relation to the Station, and heard Mr. Willard voice the anticipated response with a sinking feeling.

'Sara just suggested that we take a trip out in the morning to see her pets,' he said. 'Will that be all right with you?'

To do Steve credit he didn't even glance her way. 'Good idea. Make a change for everybody.'

'Thanks. That's settled, then.' The other indicated a spare chair. 'How about joining us for a drink?'

Expecting – or was it hoping? – for him to refuse, Sara was disconcerted when Steve accepted the invitation without hesitation and sat down in the proffered chair while their host summoned a waiter. Couldn't she even have one day free of him? she fumed, conveniently forgetting the three previous when she hadn't seen him until nightfall. He was doing it on purpose because he knew she didn't want him there, she decided, catching his mocking glance. She turned her back on him with deliberation and treated Travis to a smile which lit up his eyes in response.

'You were going to tell me what you do back home,' she said with blatant disregard for the truth.

With such encouragement she could hardly blame

Travis for taking her at her word and doing just that. He was training to be an architect, it turned out, and was totally fascinated by the whole field of learning in which he was immersed. Sara listened to him enthusiastically extolling the virtues of one style and period of building as opposed to another, learned something about the techniques employed by Wren and the manner in which these had been adapted in modern-day architecture, and tried her best to look and sound suitably impressed. What made it worse was that she could hear Steve's voice in the background casually answering questions put to him in friendly curiosity by the Willards regarding his background, and she wanted, badly, to listen in to *that* conversation with all her attention. She had a strong feeling that it wasn't very usual for Steve to be quite so forthcoming, but he apparently liked the Willards enough to bend a few personal rules. Remembering the brief, almost abrupt manner in which he had answered her own query along those lines the other night, Sara felt more than a little hurt.

When, after about half an hour, Steve finally announced that he would have to be going, she made a swift decision without waiting to be asked.

'I think I will come with you and save Temu the journey later on.'

'Then you'd better get some clothes on,' was the reply. 'And make it snappy. I've got some reports to make out before tonight's radio call.'

Smarting, she went to get her things from the little locker room she always used, sliding into jeans and shirt over the bikini and running the usual hand through her hair. When she got outside again the Willards had moved down to this end of the terrace with Steve, and were watching a herd of zebra moving down to the waterhole two hundred yards away and some twenty feet below. Chipper had disappeared during the previous conversational interlude, but he reappeared again as if by magic to remind them about the proposed visit the following day.

'We won't forget, old son,' promised Steve. 'It's all laid on.'

Sara waited until they were in the car and bouncing down the track away from the Lodge before saying tentatively, 'Thanks.'

He glanced at her and away again. 'For what?'

'You know what. For not getting on your high horse over my asking them over tomorrow.'

'Is that what you were expecting?'

'Well . . .' she made a small movement of her shoulders . . . 'you do like doing it where I'm concerned, don't you?'

He considered that for a moment before answering. 'Only when it's called for, and I don't happen to think that it was this afternoon – unless you only invited them in the hope of getting at me.'

'Of course I didn't,' she came back with alacrity. 'If I wanted to get at you I wouldn't rope anybody in to help me do it!'

He grinned. 'That I can believe. Miss Independence herself!'

Sara took a hold on her temper. He was deliberately trying to rile her, but she wasn't going to rise to it. Not this time. 'What would you prefer?' she asked sweetly.

'Wide-eyed worship?'

'Heaven preserve me!' He gave her an amused look. 'You're like a Kelly. You can be put down, but you don't stay there long. Not building up to another kick over the traces, I hope.'

'I wouldn't dream of it. We have to preserve your image.'

'Thoughtful of you. You certainly do a good enough job on your own.'

She was startled enough to reveal it. 'What does that mean exactly?'

'Exactly what it says. You got a jolt the other afternoon and you didn't like it, so once you'd got over the initial setback you immediately set out to convince me that my opinions don't matter one way or another to you.'

'That's not true!'

'Oh? Then they do matter?'

'No! At least . . .' She stopped, said crossly, 'Do you always have to be so blasted sure about everything!'

'Only when I am.' He swung the wheel. 'And don't swear. It's not ladylike.'

'According to you I'm not ladylike anyway.'

'That's not to say you can't be with a little effort. Why don't you give me a real shock tonight and come in to dinner in a dress?'

'No, thanks,' she responded after a moment. 'You'd probably have some crack ready for that too.'

'Your trouble is a suspicious mind, my girl. You want to try showing a little trust in a man's better side.'

'I might if I thought he had one.' She caught a

movement out of the corner of her eye and put a hand on his sleeve. 'Elephant.'

'I've seen them.' Steve was already slowing. He brought the car to a halt as the first great beast moved slowly out of cover, ears fanning in and out, trunk raised to quest the wind. Behind came a group of cows and young close up together, followed by a pair of young bulls who kept pushing one another like arguing schoolboys as they followed the rest across the road. One of the babies gave a squeal as its mother hurried it along with a well-aimed swing of her trunk, trotting on with its over-sized ears flattened to its skull to dissolve into the trees on the other side along with its fellows. As the last grey bulk melted silently away, Sara let out an entranced breath and turned bright eyes on her companion.

'Aren't they the most . . .'

'Quiet.' He said it softly. 'The rear-guard is just a mite close.'

There was further movement in the bush on their left, fifty feet nearer this time, and another three bulls broke cover abreast of each other to plod slowly and ponderously across the track in the wake of their companions. Last of all came one of the biggest cows Sara had ever seen, her massive head waving from side to side as she came to a full stop right on the track itself and looked directly at the car some forty feet away. It was obvious that she had got wind of them, obvious too that she didn't like the smell of them, for her trunk went up suddenly and she trumpeted, her spreading ears signalling the impending charge.

Steve restarted the engine with a quick flick of his

wrist, slammed into reverse and pushed back down the track at a steady speed, never taking his eyes off the challenging animal up ahead. The cow made a short run of a few paces, paused and trumpeted again, then shook her head as though dismissing them as hardly worth the trouble and angled off into the forest with contempt in the sway of her huge hindquarters.

'Nice to know you don't try to lord it over everything female,' remarked Sara innocently as Steve put the car into forward gear again, and he grinned.

'When they come as big as that I always give best. What were you going to say a moment ago?'

'I've forgotten,' she returned untruthfully. 'That was quite exciting.'

'Stop being so blasé. It was too damn close, and you know it. That cow could have caught us up without trying at that distance.'

'She probably didn't fancy you.' With some relish she tagged on, 'If you don't like to hear me swear you could try setting me a good example by way of a start. We kids learn by imitation.'

'So do monkeys. Incidentally,' he added before she could think of a reply to that one, 'you had young Willard really giving forth back there. How much do you know about architecture?'

'A great deal more than I did,' she admitted ruefully. 'I didn't expect a lecture on the subject.'

'That'll teach you not to cock a snook at me in future! I thought he seemed a nice boy.'

'Oh, he is!' She gave him a bright glance. 'Do you think he'd make me a good husband?'

Steve laughed. 'He wouldn't know whether he was

standing on his head or his heels after a week with you. The man you eventually marry will have to be permanently on his toes!'

'Sounds terribly uncomfortable. Seeing you know so much about it perhaps you'd pick me out a few suitable candidates when you get back to Nairobi and send them up on approval. A girl can't be too careful.' She scratched absently at a fly bite on the back of her neck, caught his amused look and desisted abruptly. 'Is Jill allowed any boy-friends?'

His brow lifted. 'Why don't you ask her when she gets here?'

'I will.' She thought about it for a moment or two, then sighed. 'Sorry. I didn't mean to be sarcastic at her expense. Does your sister have a lot of friends?'

'I'd say so. She lives with some old friends of the family in Mombasa, and as they had two young daughters of their own, plus a son, she moves in quite a large circle. Ever been down to Mombasa yourself?'

Sara nodded. 'It was quite a long time ago, though, before Dad got this job.'

'While your mother was alive?'

'Yes.'

'Still miss her?'

'It depends on how you mean it.' Her tone was careful. 'It was a long time ago, and Dad has been marvellous.'

'It might have been better for you both if he'd got married again, though,' was the judicious comment. 'A girl needs a mother as well as a father. Would you have objected?'

'Not if he'd met somebody he'd wanted to marry.

71

Anyone he'd chosen I'd have liked.'

Steve's lips twisted a little. 'Life isn't always as easy as that.'

'Well, I wouldn't have been jealous, if that's what you're suggesting. I'm not *that* self-centred.'

'Don't jump the gun. All I meant was that it isn't always possible to like someone just because someone else does. The qualities a man might look for in a woman don't have to include a strong maternal instinct.'

'Oh?' She looked at him quickly. 'Don't you like children yourself?'

'Can't say I've given it a great deal of thought. What makes you ask that?'

'The way you spoke about what a man looks for in a woman.'

'That was a qualified statement I made, not a hard and fast rule. I daresay I'd be as keen to have a couple of kids as the next chap if I got married.'

Sara made her voice deliberately light and breezy. 'But you being a confirmed bachelor, that situation is hardly likely to arise.'

His mouth pulled up at the corners. 'I never said anything about being a confirmed bachelor. Just because I've steered clear of the matrimonial bed till now it doesn't necessarily mean that I shan't take myself a wife one of these fine days. It's a pity you're not a few years older yourself. With a little training you'd probably fill the bill very nicely.'

Her heart was beating unaccountably faster, but she kept her smile steady. 'I'd probably put arsenic in your whisky before the week was up.'

72

'I don't doubt it. Nothing like living dangerously!'
He gave a mock sigh. 'Like I said, it's a pity.'

'I wish,' she said with her eyes on the road, 'that
you'd stop treating me like a twelve-year-old.'

'How would you prefer to be treated?' on a jeering
note. 'As a woman?'

Her chin came up. 'It would make a change. You
might even get an adult response!'

There was a screeching of brakes as he brought the
car to a sudden and startling halt. He turned sideways
in his seat and looked at her, one arm resting lightly
along the wheel, his expression speculative. 'All right,'
he said, 'let's be adult. Come over here.'

Sara shrank back involuntarily into her corner of the
cabin. 'Don't be ridiculous!'

'There's nothing ridiculous about a kiss between a
man and a woman,' he returned equably, and took his
arm off the wheel to reach out and draw her resistingly
towards him, holding her there in front of him with an
arm about her shoulders. With the other hand he
smoothed back the tousled hair from her forehead,
then slid his fingers down the line of her cheek and
along her lips. She saw the glint in the grey eyes as he
bent his head towards her, felt the brush of his lips at
the corner of her mouth, then he was holding her away
from him and studying her flaming cheeks with a satirical smile. 'But I don't think you're quite ready for
the full treatment yet.'

Sara's eyes were blazing. 'You . . . You . . .' she stam-
mered.

'Now don't say anything you'll be sorry for,' he ad-
vised. 'Grown-ups don't let their tongues run away

with them. Maybe next time I'll get around to taking things a little further.'

'If you touch me again *you'll* be sorry,' she managed, low-toned. 'I'll ... I'll report you to the Director!'

His grin was derisive. 'That's my girl! Never a dull moment! Are you going to behave yourself until we get back, or shall we do a little more research into this touching business here and now?'

She sat back in her seat with compressed lips, not deigning to answer. It was useless, she told herself furiously. Steve always managed to have the last word no matter what she said.

The moment they came to a stop outside the house she got out of the car without a word and went straight indoors to her own room. With the door safely closed behind her, she sat down on the bed and pressed a hand to the spot where Steve had kissed her. It had been a rotten thing to do, especially the way he had done it – leading her on to say things she didn't mean just so that he could make fun of her. She had hated it, and yet at the same time it had created a small, gnawing hunger inside her, a need to know what it would be like to be kissed properly by a man like Steve York. The full treatment, he had called it. Sara put both hands to her suddenly hot cheeks and tried to steady the almost painful thumping of her heart. This was ridiculous. She didn't even like him all that much.

She avoided him as much as possible for the rest of the day, but made a special effort at dinnertime to appear her normal unconcerned self. Once or twice she caught Steve eyeing her quizzically, but he made no comment which could be even remotely interpreted as a reference to the afternoon. Sara was glad when ten o'clock came round and she could make for her room with a plausible plea of tiredness. It wasn't until she heard Steve's voice in the corridor bidding Kimani good night, and then the click of his own door that she finally slept, however.

The Willards arrived at nine with their hired guide from the Lodge. Chipper tumbled from the Land Rover bright-eyed and brimming over with questions instantly forgotten when he saw Kiki perched on Sara's shoulder. Responding as always to attention, the little animal was not at all loth to accompany his new friend on a quick tour of the compound, showing his jealous resentment of Chipper's delight in the fawn by nipping his ear and shrieking indignantly until they came away from the pen.

While Mr. and Mrs. Willard took drinks with the three men on the veranda, Sara kept her promise to show the boys the view from the bluff. She took the field-glasses with her, and gained a gratifying response from Travis as he swept from horizon to horizon in rapt attention. Chipper was far more interested in looking for the snakes which Sara had mentioned, and terribly disappointed when he failed to find any in the immediate vicinity.

'They don't hang around if they hear you coming,' she explained. 'Poking a stick into a hole is about the quickest way of scaring them off. Anyway, we don't want you getting bitten.'

'The snake would probably come off worst,' commented his brother dryly as he leaned back against a rock. 'This is the life! I'm going to hate going back tomorrow. Another night here, then one more in Nairobi, and then home.'

'Well, you could hardly study architecture out here on a reserve,' Sara pointed out practically. 'Not unless you concentrated on mud huts and log cabins. Once you're back home you'll soon forget all this.'

'Not all of it,' he returned softly, looking at her with frankly admiring eyes. 'I've never met a girl like you before, Sara. All the kids back home think about is dressing-up and dating. I'll bet you never even bother to look in a mirror, yet you look better than most of them do after spending hours in front of one.' He caught the expression in her eyes and looked surprised. 'I can't be the first guy who ever told you you're pretty. What about all the others who've been to the Lodge?'

Sara smiled and shrugged. 'I don't go over there all that often. And I haven't noticed anybody taking any particular interest before.'

'Maybe because you froze them off before they could get started. You looked at me a bit as if I were a reptile slithering over the grass yesterday.'

'Did I?' She was startled. 'I didn't realize.'

Travis laughed. 'Oh, that's okay. It takes more than that to put me off. Pop says I lack sensitivity. Do you think I do?'

'I'd have to know you better before I answered that,' she answered on a light note.

'Not much chance of that. I'll probably never see you again after today. I don't suppose there's any chance of you coming acrosss to the States some time?'

'I don't suppose there is.' Sara wondered why she couldn't rouse herself to more enthusiasm for this conversation than she felt at the moment. Here was a very attractive and rather nice young man paying her just the kind of attention all girls were supposed to like, whether they believed it or not, and yet she might just as well have been talking to Chipper for all it meant to her. Travis was so young, and it was a well-known fact that girls were always emotionally ahead of boys in their age group. But it was more than just that, she realized. The whole atmosphere between them was lacking in any kind of excitement. Yesterday with Steve in the car, her pulses had been racing and her heart hammering into her throat before he had even touched her. Not fear, more a kind of quivering anticipation. And yet he wasn't half as nice as Travis. He bullied her, mocked her, even threatened her when he felt like it. It didn't make any sense.

She came back to earth to find Travis standing right in front of her, his face resolute. 'I don't usually have to do any asking,' he was saying, 'but I want very badly to kiss you, Sara. Are you going to let me?'

Her mouth went stiff. 'Chipper . . .'

'He's off exploring. We'll probably have to look for him when we want to go back.' He put a hand on her forearm, smiling, his face a little flushed. 'You're so different. I don't think I've ever felt quite like this about anybody before.'

She gazed at him like a child at a problem picture, not at all sure how to handle the situation. She liked Travis so much – what she knew of him – and she knew that if she said no then he'd accept it without attempting to force the issue. It was perhaps this latter fact which helped to make up her mind – that, and a certain curiosity. She smiled back suddenly. 'Why not?'

His mouth was cool and gentle and tasted of mint. Sara found the experience pleasant and somehow comforting, and felt no particular wish to stop it. Only when his arms started to tighten and his lips to move against hers did she stiffen slightly and draw back.

Travis let her go at once. He looked a bit sheepish. 'Sorry,' he murmured. 'I got a bit carried away. Haven't you been kissed before?'

'Not since I was sixteen,' she admitted. 'And the boy was the same age, so it didn't get far.' She pushed her hair back and summoned a smile. 'You don't have to be sorry, Travis. You didn't do anything out of place. We'd better look for Chipper and get back.'

Looking for Chipper proved no great difficulty. His voice came excitedly from the other side of the big rock over which he had scrambled a moment or two before. 'Hey, come and look! I've found a big one!'

'Stay away from it, Chipper!' called Sara urgently. She took a hasty step twards the voice, slipped on some loose stones and fell heavily against a jutting piece of rock at her back. There was a burning sensation under her left shoulder-blade and an arrow of pain as she pushed herself upright again, but she shook her head when Travis asked if she was hurt. 'No, I'm all right. Get to Chipper before he does something silly.'

They found the boy peering regretfully down a slit between two rocks. 'It got away. You should have seen it, Travis. Real long, it was, and thin with a funny pattern. I wonder what kind it was.'

'It could have been a lot of kinds,' said Sara steadily, pushing away the terrifying image of what it sounded like. 'You mustn't ever go too near a snake, Chipper, unless you're quite sure it's harmless. They'll nearly always get away if they can, but if they're cornered they'll defend themselves.' Her back was really hurting now and she was having difficulty in not showing it. 'Come on, it's time we were going back.'

The climb down was painful. She could feel her shirt clinging to her back and hoped that it was perspiration and not blood. She kept her back to both Travis and Chipper as much as possible as they walked through the low scrub to the fence, and for once was content to go round by the gate instead of climbing over.

Steve was still entertaining the Willards on the veranda, both Ted and Kimani having disappeared. Sara sank into a chair with her drink, concealing a wince as her back came into contact with the cane. As soon as the Willards had left she would go and see what the damage was and put something on it. It was hurting like blazes. Meanwhile she must make an effort to ignore it. She had no intention of letting Steve know that she had hurt herself.

Chipper was telling them about his encounter with the snake, reeling off its vital statistics which had just about doubled since coming down from the bluff.

'Probably a rock python,' said Steve reassuringly. 'They're quite harmless.'

'Oh?' Chipper looked positively disappointed. Sara suspected that by the time he returned to school that rock python would have become something much more

79

excitingly dangerous. She stole a glance at Steve, to have it returned expressionlessly. He knew as well as she did that it had been no rock python, and he was going to have something to say later on about letting Chipper go off like that on his own. She could read all the signs by now.

The Willards stayed a further half an hour before making a move to return to the Lodge for lunch, and an afternoon's game hunting for last-minute camera trophies. Both Mr. and Mrs. Willard were profuse in their thanks for the hospitality offered them at the Station, and Travis took no trouble to conceal his reluctance to depart, holding on to Sara's hand far longer than he needed after shaking it. Her last sight of him was of a fair head thrust through a side window and a hand waving vigorously as the car vanished among the trees beyond the compound gates.

'Nice people,' commented Steve, lighting a cigarette. 'It would have been a real pity to have ruined their whole vacation.'

'I know.' Sara was standing with her back to one of the posts, although not quite touching it. 'You don't have to say it. I should have watched him more closely.'

'I assumed you were otherwise occupied.' He said it dryly. 'You seem to have knocked young Willard for six.'

'How British,' she mocked back deliberately.

'Cricket isn't confined to the British Isles,' he came back equally deliberately. 'What game does friend Travis play?'

'A fair one. He doesn't try to take advantage of a novice!'

His mouth pulled into a slow smile. 'You may be a novice in some things, but when it comes to answering back you're an expert. One of these days you'll . . .' He broke off as she eased herself away from the post, catching the flicker of pain across her face. 'What's wrong?'

'Nothing.' She looked him straight in the eye. 'I'm a bit stiff from climbing.'

'Like hell you are!' He whipped out a hand and caught her by the wrist, turning her sideways so that he could see the back of her shirt. 'There's blood coming through. What the devil have you been up to now?'

'Don't bark,' she snapped peevishly. 'I told you it was nothing. I slipped and fell against the rock. It's just a graze. I'm going to put something on it now.'

'And how do you think you're going to see to do it?' with sarcasm. He let her go. 'Come on inside and I'll have a look at it.'

'I wouldn't let you touch me with a barge-pole,' she said between her teeth. 'I can manage, thanks.'

He said something explosively under his breath, and then out loud, 'I'm not asking you I'm telling you! Now get inside and get that shirt off while I fetch a first-aid kit.'

She was still standing where he had left her in the doorway when he came back with the box. He gave her an exasperated look and nodded towards the nearest hard-backed chair. 'For God's sake, you can sit with your back to me if you're that modest. I saw you in just as little at the Lodge yesterday.'

'No, you didn't.' She tried to say it matter-of-factly.

'I'm only wearing this at the moment.'

His lips twisted faintly. 'It figures. So what?'

'So I'm not taking my shirt off. I daresay life holds nothing new for you, but I've had a sheltered up-bringing.' Despite everything she could do to stop it her voice quivered just a little on the last word. 'Let me do my own first-aid.'

'You won't be able to see properly. It looks as though you've cut or grazed yourself right under the shoulder blades. Lie on your stomach on your bed if you must, but one way or another I'm going to take a look at that back. Right?'

She gave in. There was nothing else she could do. With her head up she walked past him and along the corridor to her own room, took off the shirt and sat down on the edge of the bed with her back to the door and the garment held stubbornly across her front. When he came into the room she didn't look at him.

Steve took one glance at the slender tanned back presented to him and whistled softly between his teeth. 'That's some graze! It must be giving you gyp. You're going to need some kind of dressing on it until it stops oozing blood. At least it's clean.'

Sara felt the mattress sag as he sat down just behind her and opened the first-aid box, and then the light, spine-tingling touch of his fingers and the bite of anti-septic. Her lower lip caught between her teeth, she sat there motionless while he dressed and taped the wounded area. She could feel the faint stirring of his breath on the back of her neck among the tendrils of hair which curled into her nape. She wanted desperately to say something to break the silence, but she couldn't think of a single thing. She had never been more relieved in her life when the last piece of sticking plaster was in place.

'There,' he said. 'All done and dusted. Wasn't so bad, was it?'

'No,' she managed on a reasonably even note.

He ran the back of a knuckle over her nape, the kind of gesture she could imagine him making to his sister Jill in one of his softer moods. It was something to cling to at a moment when her emotions were in such a state of confusion. He was simply being brotherly.

'It's going to stiffen up when it starts to skin over,' he added, getting to his feet. 'Nothing much we can do about that.' There was a brief pause before he tagged on satirically, 'At least it should keep you out of mischief for a day or two. You can get dressed again now.'

Sara waited until the door had closed behind him, then she got up herself and went over to the wardrobe, twisting her neck to study his handiwork. The dressing was neat and quite extensive. Steve had been right about one thing, she wouldn't have been able to do much with it on her own. She looked dispassionately at her reflection, still holding the shirt to her. It hadn't meant a thing to him seeing her like this. She could have sat there without a stitch on and it still wouldn't have meant a thing to him. She was just a kid it amused him to taunt on occasion, and that was all. She'd better keep telling herself that.

# CHAPTER FOUR

THERE was a letter from Sara's father a couple of days later, backing up the telegram he had sent immediately on landing in London. The weather was terrible, he said, but matters were well in hand. He was going to spend a few days with some old friends in the country, perhaps get in some fishing if the rain stopped. London hadn't changed all that much. There was more traffic on the streets, of course, and a few familiar landmarks had disappeared for ever, but essentially it was still the same old place. He doubted that Benston would have altered at all in the years since he had last been there. He certainly hoped not. At one time he had intended to retire there.

'You are missing your father?' asked Kimani, coming across her gazing into space with the letter still open in her hand.

He had approached quietly, and Sara started, looking up from her seat on the steps to meet his smiling regard. 'What . . . Well, yes, I am, I suppose. He seems to have been gone an age.'

'You should have gone with him,' he said, taking a seat beside her and lighting a cigarette. 'He would have enjoyed your company, and you the change of scene.'

'If one more person tells me I need a change from here . . .' began Sara, then paused and added wryly, 'Sorry. Didn't mean to snap your head off, Kim. I think I'm starting to lose my sense of humour.'

'You're bored,' he returned frankly. 'Perhaps when Steve's young sister arrives things will be better. Have you heard yet when she's due?'

'No. He hasn't mentioned it since that first time. When did he tell you about it?'

'A few days ago. The supply plane is due on Friday. She may be coming through on that.'

'I suppose so.' Sara still wasn't at all sure that she wanted the other girl here. She wasn't sure of anything these days. She changed the subject. 'Are you going out today?'

'Soon. Do you want to come along?'

'Depends where you're going.'

His teeth flashed white against copper skin. 'Buffalo hunting. Is that exciting enough for you?'

'Might be. Mind if I drive?'

His shrug was good-humoured. 'Why not? A man can only die once.'

She pulled a face at him, sticking the letter in her pants' pocket as she got up. She would write back to-night although it wouldn't go till Friday now. She should have had one written ready to give to the Willards to post for her in Nairobi, she thought. They would be half-way there by this time. She wondered if Travis was thinking of her.

They took one of the rangers with them, plus a packed lunch, and drove out in the direction of the Escarpment for ten miles or so before branching off into the bush in search of the shy but exceedingly dangerous black buffalo. Kimani had seen two separate herds of the animals in the area a few days previously and wanted to check on their direction and progress.

It took them almost two hours to find one herd, and even then they could easily have missed them if Kimani hadn't spotted one of the sentry bulls on the edge of a thicket. He took the car downwind, and left Sara in it while he and Temu moved up cautiously on the main body of the herd to do a count. She watched them through the glasses for a few minutes until the bush hid them from her view, then settled herself down resignedly to wait for their reappearance.

There was a herd of Thomson's gazelle about five hundred yards away, grazing peacefully and flicking their tails. Sara watched idly, not really thinking about anything very much until a movement in the grass roughly half-way between the car and the herd brought her alert. There was some animal creeping up on the gazelles, trying to get as close as possible before attacking. She caught a glimpse of spotted fur and a small head. Cheetah! One of the few predators which hunted by day, and the fastest in action. Whichever animal had been singled out as prey didn't stand much of a chance if the big cat got within striking distance without discovery.

But now the herd was alerted, the sentry animals on the outer edge facing outwards in the direction of the advancing menace, bodies tensed, heads lifted to assess the nature of the threat. The cheetah broke cover with a bound which carried it several yards across the expanse of shorter grass between it and the herd, and then it was running smoothly and at top speed on the heels of the fleeing herd, ignoring all but the one animal it had set its sights on. It was all over in seconds. A streak of silver as the cat launched itself at the neck of its prey, and the gazelle was down, the rest of the drama hidden in the scrub.

The shots came at almost the same moment, two of them close together. Without stopping to consider, Sara grabbed the spare gun and made in the direction of the sound, ignoring the snatch of branch and twig at her clothing as she pressed into the bush along the narrow game trail the two men had taken some minutes before. She came upon them quite suddenly, to find Temu kneeling above the prostrate figure of Kimani Ngogi, while not ten feet away lay the body of a full-grown bull buffalo, its magnificent spread of horns completely blocking the trail.

Kimani was conscious but obviously in pain, his right leg doubled under him at a crazy angle. The bull had come at them totally unexpectedly from the flank, forcing him to shoot in self-defence. When his shot failed to stop the bull he had given it the other barrel and then leaped to one side to avoid the impetus of its rush even as it died on its feet. In doing so he had fallen heavily, and clearly heard the bone crack as it twisted under him.

'You're going to have to splint it and help me out of here, you and Temu,' he said stoically.

Sara stayed with him while Temu made for the nearest tree several hundred yards away and lopped off a couple of the straightest branches he could find. Getting the broken limb straightened out was the worst part of the job. Kimani's face was beaded in sweat by the time his leg was securely bound to the improvised splints with strips torn from Temu's shirt. Hoisting him to his feet proved no easy task either, but they managed it. With the young Kenyan hitched firmly if agonizingly over Temu's broad shoulders the little party set off back to the car, Sara walking in front with the gun at the ready for trouble from any quarter. She was highly relieved when they reached their destination without meeting any.

There wasn't room in the back of the Rover to lay Kimani flat, but by a dint of manoeuvring they managed to get him sitting between the seats with his injured leg stretched out before him. There was blood on his lower lip where his teeth had bitten in during the gruelling moments of being carried here. Sara wished with all her heart that they had something to give him strong enough to ease the pain, but the first-aid kits in the car carried no morphine, even if she had known how to go about administering it.

She deliberately turned her back on him as Temu slipped into the driving seat and started the engine, knowing how much his Masai blood would resent the indignity of having a woman witness his helplessness.

He passed out at least twice during the fifty-minute journey back to Kambala, his head lolling back against the partition. Sara felt each bump and jolt with him, although Temu did his best to pick out as level a route as possible. Never had the sight of the Station been so welcome.

Steve was still out on patrol, and not expected back before nightfall. With Temu and another of the rangers carrying him into the house, Kimani was made as comfortable as possible on the bed in his room while

Ted radioed for help. When he came back he told them that a plane was being sent out immediately to transport the injured man back to civilization for proper care and attention.

'But we still have to get him across to the airstrip,' Sara said worriedly. 'That's another hour's journey, and he's almost exhausted with pain now.'

'We've got morphine,' Ted reassured her. 'I've given it before in an emergency. You'd better stay on here and tell Steve what's happened if he does get back early.'

Half an hour later the car was on its way again, travelling at its normal steady pace with Kimani as comfortable as he could be in the back. Sara watched it out of sight before turning back disconsolately into the house. It had all happened so quickly; there had been no real time in which to think about it up till this moment. Now she realized for the first time that she had probably seen the last of Kimani Ngogi, if not for good, then certainly for a good length of time. The Department would probably send someone else out to finish off the present phase of his work. It was going to seem odd without the young Kenyan around the place. More than anything would she miss his unfailing good humour and readiness to allow her to share in his work.

The afternoon wore on. Ted still hadn't returned when the other Land-Rover came slowly up the track. Steve climbed from behind the wheel, tossing his hat back into the cabin and stretching as he looked up the steps to where Sara stood in the shade.

'You're looking very solemn and serious,' he remarked. 'Is that what my homecoming does to you?'

'Kim broke a leg,' she stated baldly. 'He'll be on his way to Nairobi by now.'

The smile faded from his face. 'How did it happen?'

She told him, and he shook his head. 'Lucky it wasn't worse. He should have known better than to follow buffalo into thick bush. How about a drink?'

Sara followed him into the living-room, standing in the doorway as he moved across to the cabinet. 'Is that all it means to you?' she demanded.

He turned to consider her for a moment. 'Now what are you on about?'

'Kim could have been killed, and all you can say is that he should have known better!'

'Well, what am I supposed to say?'

'A little sympathy is usual.'

'What good is that to him when he isn't even here? Come to think of it, what good would it be to him if he were here?' He finished pouring the whisky, splashed in some orange and looked back at her with faintly curling lip. 'How's the back?'

'All right.' Her voice was short.

'From which I gather that you've no intention of letting me touch it again. Okay, no reason why I should unless it starts going the wrong way, and that seems unlikely.' He sat down in the nearest chair, slinging a leg over the arm and taking a long pull from his glass. 'That's better!' Grey eyes slid her way when she failed to make any move, and a hint of impatience came into his expression. 'Either sit down and be sociable or run away and play with your toys,' he exclaimed. 'What the devil's wrong with you, anyway?'

Sara couldn't have told him with any certainty herself. All she did know was that the tensions which had been slowly building up inside her over the last couple of days had reached eruption point on seeing him walk so unconcernedly past her a moment ago. Nothing touched him. There was no softness in him at all. She wanted desperately to hurt him, and didn't know how.

'There's nothing wrong with *me*,' she answered. 'I just don't like having the people and things I care about dismissed as if they were of no consequence. I don't suppose you made a mistake in your life!'

'I've made plenty,' was the even response. 'But never the same one twice. Cut it out, will you?'

'Or what?' she flung at him recklessly. 'You'll send me to bed without any supper? Do you act the heavy father with Jill too?'

'Not since she was fourteen. And I said cut it out.'

'Go to hell!'

It hardly needed the ominous tautening of his jaw to tell her that this time she had gone too far, but having said it she wasn't going to retract. There was a bare moment's silence while he sat there studying her narrowly, then he put down the glass and got purposefully to his feet.

'You asked for it.'

Sara stood her ground for all of three seconds as he moved towards her, before turning abruptly to dive across the veranda and down the steps into the compound. Her heart thudded as she heard him jump the steps behind her, but she kept on going round the corner of the house and across the grass to vault the fence at its nearest point and make for the belt of trees. Afterwards she told herself that she should have known Steve York wouldn't give up that easily. When she reached the trees he was on her heels, and before she had taken another dozen steps he had her by the belt of her jeans, yanking her to a standstill and jerking her round to face him.

At that moment she went wild, kicking out at him with both feet, pummelling him with her fists, twisting fiercely in an effort to break his hold on her. His hand loosened its grasp on her belt, but only to slide around her waist and lift her bodily from the ground. Pinned against his chest, she found herself looking straight into the glinting grey eyes.

'Now what have you to say for yourself?' he demanded.

'Put me down!' She could scarcely breathe, but she still had the use of her feet, and didn't much care where they landed. She saw him wince as one toecap connected sharply with his shinbone, and knew a moment's vicious delight. Then he grabbed her by the knees and swung her round in his arms so that she lay with her head against his shoulder, holding her there with a grip that hurt.

'I somehow don't think it'd do much good to paddle you,' he said mockingly. 'But there's more than one way to skin a cat!'

His mouth found hers, parting her lips to a bruising merciless kiss. She fought him savagely, but she was helpless against his strength and purpose. And then the fight went out of her, leaving her quivering unresisting in his arms. When he lifted his head again she could feel the heat flooding her cheeks and knew that he must be aware of the mad pounding of her heart. In that moment she hated him with everything that was in her.

'That will perhaps teach you to curb that tongue of yours,' he said with satire. 'All through, are we?'

'Let me go.' Her voice sounded thick.

'Sure.' He set her back on her feet and stood to one side to indicate the way they had come. 'Ladies first.'

Sara walked past him, only too conscious that he was laughing at her. She wanted to kill him, not so much for what he had done but for the way he had done it. She wished suddenly and passionately that she were older, sophisticated, capable of taking an incident like that in her stride – except that if she had been it wouldn't have happened, at least not in the same way.

The car was coming up the track as she rounded the corner of the house again with Steve a few feet behind her. Ted wasn't alone in it. A dark head showed beside him, and an arm was stuck out through the side window eagerly waving. Sara heard Steve exclaim something, then he was passing her and striding on to greet the slim, vivacious girl who almost fell out of the door into his arms.

'Surprise!' she cried gaily. 'They told us this plane was coming through, so we rallied round and made it. Isn't it marvellous that Don and Diane could come too?'

Steve released her and turned his gaze on the couple

who had emerged from the back of the vehicle, his smile altering subtly as his eyes met those of the tall, auburn-haired young woman in the beautifully tailored beige trousers and shirt. 'Unexpected,' he said. 'I never thought to find you taking a trip out here, Diane.'

Her answering smile was slow and confident, accentuating the planes and angles of her thin, arresting features. 'I never thought to find myself doing it, but curiosity overcame reluctance. We're booked in at the Lodge for a few nights. Do you think you'll be able to spare some time to show us the sights?'

'I daresay.' He looked from her to the man at her side. 'Are you here because you want to be or because you were dragged?'

'Because I was too idle to think up an adequate get-out,' came the easy response. 'How about introducing us to your young friend?'

Until that moment Sara had been unaware that she was standing staring at the small group. Now, as Steve turned his head to glance back at her, she went hot again, with embarrassment this time. She must seem very gauche to these newcomers.

'Sara Macdonald,' he said evenly. 'The daughter of the permanent warden here. Come on over, Sara, and meet the Milsons.'

'And me,' chimed in his sister indignantly. She smiled at Sara, blue-grey eyes sparkling. 'We're the same age, I gather.'

'Yes.' Sara could think of nothing further to add. Jill York might be her age, but on first sight that was about the only thing they had in common. She was so pretty even in jeans and shirt, her dark brown hair layered into a shining pageboy bob which reached almost to her shoulders. Between her and Diane Milson Sara felt shabby, gauche and totally unfeminine.

If Jill was thinking the same she gave no sign of it. 'Steve told us you'd lived out here since you left school,' she said. 'I'm afraid you're going to have to put up with almost complete ignorance from me. I can't tell a grass snake from a puff-adder!'

Sara had to smile back. 'It won't matter,' she returned, sticking her hands in her pockets. 'I'm sure your brother can.'

Don Milson grinned suddenly. 'Meaning that you're not going to get far without him, Jill.' His gaze resting on Sara was speculative and amused. 'I gather our friend here has been laying down the law since he arrived. Tends to do that with the fair sex, I've noticed. Keeps 'em under control like the rest of the game.'

'Shut up,' said Diane pleasantly, and then to Sara, 'You have to take my brother as you find him, I'm afraid. His manners aren't all they should be.'

So the Milsons were brother and sister. Sara had thought them husband and wife. She could feel Steve's eyes on her, but nothing would have persuaded her to look at him right then. 'Why don't we all go indoors?' she suggested brightly, determined to regain at least a little of the initiative in her own home. 'You must all be ready for a drink.'

'Best suggestion I've heard yet.' Don moved forward to join her. 'Lead on.'

When he set himself out, Sara found over the following minutes, Don Milson could charm the birds down from the trees. Perhaps two or three years younger than Steve, his attraction lay in the irrepressible humour lurking deep in his eyes, belying the slightly cynical cast of his features. The very fact that a man like this could find her entertaining enough to pay so much attention to was balm to her bruised spirit. She responded sparklingly, ignoring Steve's sardonic observation.

It was Ted who eventually put the suggestion forward that the Milsons should stay on at Kambala for the few days they intended to spend away from the farm they ran together.

'We do have two rooms spare now that Kimani's gone,' he pointed out. 'That is if Miss Milson doesn't mind sharing.'

It was hard to calculate Steve's reaction from his expression. He drew deeply on his cigarette before answering, exhaled slowly into the still air. 'Better if the two girls share,' he said, and to Sara, 'Any objections?'

What objection she could possibly make with the subject under discussion sitting right across from her, Sara quite failed to see and never doubted that he was perfectly aware of it himself. She met Jill's eyes and smiled. 'Not at all. There's plenty of room for another bed.'

'Fair enough.' He nodded to Ted. 'You'd better send Temu across for the baggage. He'll do it before nightfall if he leaves now.' He lifted his glass towards Diane, mouth slanting into an odd little smile. 'We can't offer you all the home comforts of the Lodge, I'm afraid.'

'But I'm sure there are compensations,' was the soft reply.

Sara was sure of it too, and the knowledge was like a sudden lead weight in her chest. When she looked up Don was watching her with a shrewd expression. She gave him a hastily contrived smile, and welcomed the diversion created by Kiki appearing on the windowsill at her shoulder.

Jill was enchanted by the gregarious little animal, and only too eager to have him perched on her shoulder while he ate the banana Sara gave him. Diane watched her young friend tolerantly, shaking her head when invited to touch the soft fur herself.

'Monkeys always make me feel itchy,' she confessed. 'I hope it doesn't get into the bedrooms.'

'He doesn't have to come indoors at all while you're here,' put in Steve before Sara could answer. 'I'm sure every effort will be made to keep him under control.' This last accompanied by a glance which challenged Sara to argue with that statement. 'They're amusing little beasts, but they can sometimes become a nuisance. Why don't you take Jill along and show her where she's going to sleep?'

His sister pulled a face at him. 'Trying to get me out of the way already?'

He smiled back. 'Not so as you'd notice. You two can start getting to know one another quicker on your own.'

Sara stood up, avoiding his eyes. 'He's probably right. Come on, Jill, let's make the most of it.'

Ted had obviously looked in on the kitchen quarters while passing, for Njorogi was already at work setting up a trestle bed beside Sara's own. He greeted their appearance with his usual flashing grin, deftly shaking a pillow into its clean case and laying it neatly at the head of the bed.

'We'll finish the rest ourselves, thank you,' said Sara firmly in Swahili, and started to unfold the sheets as the door closed behind him. 'Njorogi makes a bed beautifully, only he takes simply ages getting each sheet and blanket dead centre before he'll even start tucking in. If you find your things arranged in tidy rows along the dressing-table you'll know who's been at work. It's almost an obsession with him. My father sometimes measures the spaces between items Njorogi has tidied up, and he says there's never more than fractional difference.'

'He sounds quite a character,' Jill laughed. 'Diane is always grumbling about her house servants. You'll have to watch her or she'll be stealing him away from you.'

'Have you known the Milsons long?' Sara asked carefully as she tucked in the corners.

'About three months. Steve met them first, and then they invited both of us to spend a few weeks with them. We'd only been there a week when the Department contacted him about this job.'

Sara glanced at the other girl quickly. 'But he didn't have to take it if he was on leave.'

'Apparently they had no one else available, and Steve always did have a weakness for the highlands.' Jill was sitting on the other bed watching Sara work without it apparently having occurred to her to offer to help. 'It's certainly a much pleasanter climate than we get down at the coast. Mombasa is so humid at this time of the year.'

'Do you like Nairobi?'

'Very much. As a matter of fact there's a chance that we'll be moving there ourselves quite shortly. Steve has an eye on the farm across the valley from Don and Diane's.'

Sara frowned down at the corner she had just made. 'I wouldn't have thought him exactly ready for settling down just yet.'

'Oh, I don't know. He's always said that a man should be able to pack enough living into his first thirty-odd years to last him a lifetime, and he's certainly moved around enough.' She grimaced. 'I wish he would buy this place so that we could see a little more of each other. I usually only get to be with him for about a third of each year.'

'I gather you get along very well with your brother.'

'Yes.' Jill's gaze was suddenly a little curious. 'Correct me if I'm wrong, but I get the distinct impression that you don't like him very much.'

Was what she felt for Steve York anything at all to do with liking? Sara wondered confusedly. There was certainly nothing simple about the reactions he drew from her. 'He's only been here a bit more than a fortnight,' she protested. 'I barely know him. Perhaps I do find him a bit . . . managing.'

'Yes, I suppose he is,' with a laugh. 'Diane calls him an overbearing brute to his face, but she's the first to admit that it's one of the things which attracts her to him. Don't you think she's gorgeous?'

'I would have said beautiful in an unusual way.'

Sara kept her voice carefully expressionless. 'Are she and Steve . . . I mean, do you think he'll marry her?'

'Who knows? He's had plenty of other women friends as good-looking as Diane, but never one who kept his interest as long. She's so cool and casual. You're never quite sure what she's thinking.'

'You really do admire her, don't you?'

'Yes, I do.' A faint frown touched the vivacious features. 'On the other hand, I'm not at all sure that I'd like to have her for a sister-in-law.'

'Any particular reason?'

'Yes.' A grin overcame the frown. 'Vanity. When Diane is around nobody else gets a look in. She's one of those people who only has to walk into a room to become the centre of attention.' She gave the trestle bed a doubtful look as Sara stood back from her task. 'It's rather low. Are you sure it's safe?'

'Quite.' Sara met the blue-grey regard and added resignedly, 'You can have mine, if you like, and I'll take this.'

'Are you sure?' The question was purely rhetorical. 'I do like to sleep next to a window I must admit.' She tested the springing, then got to her feet and wandered across to the dressing-table. 'Is this your father?' she asked, picking up the framed photograph.

'Yes.'

'You're a lot like him.'

'Yes,' Sara said again, 'so I'm told. Shall we go and get your luggage out of the car? You'll want to unpack.'

'Oh, there's plenty of time for that.' Jill was at the window now, looking up towards the bluff. 'What do you find to do with yourself all day? Surely entertainment is a little restricted?'

'Not noticeably before your brother arrived,' Sara replied dryly. 'I'm sure he'll find time to take you around once your friends have gone.'

'It's to be hoped that he'll find time to take us *all* out with him,' came the ready reply. 'Don brought his ciné equipment.' She paused, her tone changing subtly. 'There's another unusual character. Outwardly he always appears so uncaring, yet underneath . . .' She stopped there, added obliquely, 'He was married once, but his wife ran off with another man.'

'Did Diane live with them then?' ventured Sara.

'I don't know. I suppose so. They're brother and sister, and like Steven and me they don't have any other family. Mind you, Diane is pretty self-sufficient. I don't imagine it would worry her if she did have to live alone for any reason.'

But it would worry Jill, Sara surmised, and the other girl recognized the fact that Diane Milson would not want *any* other female claiming too much attention from the man she had set her sights on. If she married Steve his sister could quite well find herself pushed to one side. And it was for Jill's sake alone, Sara told herself swiftly, that she felt so concerned at the thought of that marriage taking place.

Njorogi brought in Jill's case some few minutes later. Sara left her to unpack on her own and went out again to the living-room, to find Don Milson the sole occupant. Steve had taken Diane on a brief tour of the compound, he informed her.

'Didn't you want to go with them?' Sara inquired

innocently, and received a satirical grin in reply.

'Never heard the saying two's company? Di would have chopped my legs from under me if I'd even looked like getting up. Have you and Jill got yourselves sorted out?'

'Just about. She's unpacking. Can I get you another drink, Mr. Milson?'

He looked amused. 'What's wrong with Don?'

Her own lips tilted involuntarily. 'All right then, would you like another drink, Don?'

'I'd rather have your company.' He patted the seat beside him. 'Come and tell me about yourself.'

'I thought I already did that.'

'Ah, but that was a basic rundown in company. I want to know about the girl who came stalking round the corner of the house with a man hot on her heels. Had Steve been doing something he shouldn't?'

'No.' The denial was too quick; she could see that by his smile and the flick of his eyebrow. 'We'd just been having a few words, that's all,' she tagged on hastily. 'He thinks I'm still in rompers!'

'Shortsighted of him. I'd say that you'd a whole lot more poise and sense than many girls your age I could think of. The life you've led out here for the last few years is bound to have made you more independent, for one thing. That's probably what he objects to,' on a dry note. 'In Steve's book women do as they're told when it's for their own good.'

'Including your sister?' she asked after a moment.

'Sure. Di's no fool when it comes to playing up to male vanity. She'll accept things from Steve York that any other man would get flattened for even attempting to put across.'

Sara said with care, 'Does that mean she's in love with him?'

Don laughed. 'About that now I wouldn't exactly know. Di got past the habit of confiding her feelings in me a long time ago – if she ever did it. I'd say she's definitely attracted, and interested enough to make this trip against her natural instincts. My sister is more of a hothouse type than an outdoor plant. She's out of her element here and she knows it, but that doesn't stop her from playing the game through to the end. If she really does decide to want Steve then she's even capable of changing her whole life-style to get him. Anyway, that's enough about those two. I'd rather talk about us.'

'Us?'

'You and me.' He was watching her with a smile which taunted yet somehow failed to grate as it did when Steve looked at her like that. 'We are going to be friends, I hope.'

Sara felt her pulses quicken involuntarily. Don Milson was undoubtedly a very attractive man, and unlike Steve he obviously didn't see her as a mere child. Without having to think about it she found the right note of response.

'It all depends what friendship with you entails.'

The smile widened appreciatively. 'Just as much as you want it to – or as little. I'm a man content to follow where others lead. Perhaps you could show me where to get the best camera shots, for a start.'

The other were coming back, Sara could hear Diane laughing as they mounted the steps. She gave Don a wide smile. 'I'd be pleased to try.'

The day slipped into night almost unnoticed. Temu came back from the Lodge with the Milson's luggage about seven, and Diane retired to her room to change from the clothes in which she had travelled. When she appeared in the living-room just before dinner she was wearing an expensively simple linen dress in a pale shimmering green which was wonderful with her hair. Sara was suddenly glad that Jill had only bothered to change her shirt. For the first time she began to see the desirability of looking feminine on occasion, although she could never hope to come anywhere near Diane in sheer eye-catching appeal, she told herself firmly.

She missed Kimani's presence on the veranda that night after the meal. By now he would be safely in hospital with his leg properly set and at ease. From her usual seat by the rail she found herself watching Diane as she talked with the men, admiring the easy manner which seemed quite unaware of anything beyond the conversation in hand at the moment. Yet the other couldn't fail to have noticed how Steve's glance lingered on her lips as she talked, how the slight smile came and went around the corners of his own mouth as if at memories conjured up by the very sight of that full redness. When he kissed Diane it would be nothing like the way he had kissed her that afternoon, she thought, and pressed herself suddenly and abruptly to her feet.

'I haven't seen to the animals yet,' she announced to no one in particular.

'I'll come with you.' It was Don who spoke, voice casual. 'I need to stretch my legs before bed.'

He waited until they were out of earshot of the others before saying, 'Is this how you spend all your free time out here, just sitting and talking?'

'I suppose it is,' answered Sara after a moment. 'Most of it, anyway.' She glanced at him in the moonlight. 'Are you bored?'

'Already?' he added for her with a smile. 'No, but I'm surprised that you're not. I'll tell you one thing, Jill isn't going to prove too adaptable to changing conditions.'

'What does that mean exactly?'

'Simply that she's used to leading a fairly full life one way or another. She's a live wire, is our Jilly. More so than I think Steve realizes.'

'But she seemed so pleased to be here this afternoon.'

'It's a novelty to her – and she'd welcome any chance to see something of him for a change. How long is he expecting her to stay?'

'I'm not sure. Perhaps until my father comes back in about a month's time.'

'Then he's going to have to work in it.'

'I don't really see that there's so much he could do,' she commented reasonably. 'After a day in the open the men never seem to want to do anything but get their feet up with a drink.' She waited just a bare moment before adding casually, 'Is he so different away from here?'

'Well, he certainly doesn't seem against organized entertainment.' His tone was thoughtful. 'Maybe Di will start having second thoughts about him on this trip. I certainly don't see her putting her feet up night after night, even for Steve York.'

Sara couldn't either. But Steve wasn't planning on doing this kind of job for much longer according to his sister. Obviously Don didn't know that, but how about Diane? With that knowledge in mind she could afford to put up with a few days of boredom just to make sure that Steve didn't forget.

Don waited outside the pen while Sara bedded the fawn down for the night. When she let herself out again he was smoking a cigarette and listening to the night sounds.

'I once heard a recording of all this,' he said. 'I never really believed it was all genuine track until now. Is it always the same?'

'No, it can get noisier,' she smiled. 'The baboons are rather quiet tonight. Now when they get going it's a real racket!'

'Well, let's hope that nothing disturbs them.' He leaned against a fence post, reminding her of that first night Steve had been here. 'No immediate hurry to get back, is there? Stay and talk for a bit.'

'They'll be wondering where we've got to,' she hedged.

'Let 'em wonder. Do 'em good. For my part, I promise to curb my natural inclinations and refrain from molesting you.'

She looked at him uncertainly, saw his grin and relaxed suddenly. 'What a relief! I believed you might be what the magazines call a fast worker.'

'Don't you believe all you read about men, honey,' he jeered. 'Things aren't always what they seem to be.'

'No?' Guilelessly she added, 'Jill thinks you're probably not half as cynical as you make out.'

'Does she now?' He sounded faintly surprised. 'I didn't know she'd given any time to considering it one way or the other. What else did she have to say about me?'

'Only that you've been married and . . .' Sara caught herself up, aware of already having said too much.

'And?' he prompted. 'I'm sure she didn't leave it hanging in mid-air like that.'

'Well, no. She said your wife had . . . gone away.'

'That's a polite way of putting it. The usual version is "found herself another man".'

Something in his tone drew Sara's eyes to his face. 'Isn't that what happened?' He was silent for so long that she felt herself flushing. 'Sorry,' she offered. 'I shouldn't have asked. It's none of my business.'

'That's all right. I invited it.' He flicked ash from the end of his cigarette. 'Sometimes it's easiest to let people think the obvious, but the truth of the matter is that Caroline left me because she resented Diane living with us.'

'Couldn't Diane have found a place of her own?' she asked hesitantly.

'I suppose she could, but why should she have? The farm is half hers, which makes the house half hers too. I could hardly ask her to leave under the circumstances, only Caro wouldn't see it that way.' He made a small sound of disgust. 'Women!' He was silent for a few seconds, then he threw down the remains of the cigarette and trod it beneath his heel. 'That's a fine subject to get on to. Let's leave it that there were probably faults on both sides. It's been water under the bridge for the last five years.'

Sara was only too glad to leave the subject, only too sorry that she had brought it up in the first place. Don had been badly hurt in the past, and was obviously regretting this brief invasion of his privacy. So she would forget it as he said, together with the small voice which deplored the total insensitivity of a woman who would see her only brother's marriage falter on the rocks rather than make a small sacrifice herself – if she could forget that part.

She thought that Steve eyed the two of them a little sharply when they got back to the house, but he said nothing. When a few minutes later Jill professed herself unusually tired with the events of the day and the change in the air, she was almost glad of the excuse to suggest an early night for them both and accompany the other girl to the room they were to share.

Later, lying in the narrow bed while Jill breathed evenly and deeply in the other, Sara listened to the soft murmur of voices drifting in through the opened window from along the veranda, and imagined Steve out there alone with Diane; two adult people who both knew exactly what they wanted from life. They were well suited, she had to admit.

# CHAPTER FIVE

HAVING Jill and the Milsons around certainly made a difference to life at Kambala, Sara found over the following couple of days. Even Ted so far bestirred himself as to don a cravat of sorts at dinner time instead of appearing as usual in the comfortable old open-necked shirts he favoured. Sara herself got no further from her normal attire than glancing irresolutely once or twice through her wardrobe, hating to admit to herself that she envied the gay little dresses in which Jill appeared every evening. Very little of what she possessed would even fit her now, she realized, and what did was hardly in the same class. Even three years ago she hadn't been all that interested in clothes.

The whole party went out each day in one car, leaving Ted to look after the Station as always. Steve was excellent at finding game, of course, murmuring 'Couple of jackal off there to the right,' or 'Lions left of that boulder there,' long before anyone else had noticed anything at all. They were days of cruising slowly and steadily across savannah and plain, sometimes through grass deep enough to almost cover the car completely, at others over burned areas which appeared devoid of life of any kind. On the second day they spent a whole hour watching a large herd of giraffe on the edge of the forest, and being watched back with the same wide-eyed curiosity until a sudden impatient movement on Diane's part sent them cantering off with that oddly unco-ordinated motion which was so much a part of their charm.

So far as Diane was concerned it was soon obvious that the real bright spots in the days were the noon hours spent at the Lodge where she could shine in her own particular fashion. Unlike Don, she found the endless parade of wild life boring and repetitive, although she accepted the ordeal with amazing good humour. Whatever her faults, Sara decided, watching the striking, bikini-clad figure climbing from the pool, one had to admire Diane. She herself would have given a great deal for just a little of the other's unfailing self-confidence in circumstances so far removed from her normal mode of life.

Don surfaced a few feet away from her dangling legs, pausing to tread water and toss the hair out of his eyes before hauling himself out of the pool and sprawling on the grass at her side.

'I must be out of condition,' he panted. 'I feel decidedly winded after that last couple of lengths. Are you going in again?'

'I don't think so.' Sara's eyes were on Steve, standing on the far side with Diane laughing over some shared joke. His body above the white trunks was bronzed and superbly fit, with not an ounce of spare flesh in sight. She looked round quickly at Don. 'I thought Jill was with you.'

'She was, until that young Frenchy came and took her off right under my nose. She's having a tête-à-tête with him on the terrace right at this moment over a pot of coffee – or that's what he suggested, I think. My French is strictly of the schoolboy variety. I don't suppose you've got a cigarette on you.'

Sara laughed. 'Do I look as if I might have a cigarette on me – even if I smoked in the first place?'

'Well no, I suppose not,' considering her with a practised eye. 'There'd hardly be room in that suit.' He gave a mock sigh. 'I'd give a great deal to be nineteen again, with everything in front of me.'

'Do you think things would be any different?' she ventured.

'It depends. If I'd met someone like you they might have stood a better chance. I have a strong notion that when you fall in love it will be for keeps, regardless of any outside influence.' His voice lightened deliberately. 'Would you call thirty too old for a new start?'

'Hardly.'

'I'm glad you're so certain. It gives me renewed hope.' He stood up, extending his hand to pull her to her feet beside him. 'Let's get changed and have a drink before we get back on the trail.'

It was gone four when they got back to Kambala that afternoon. Diane went straight to her room to get out of the dusty and creased garments in which she had spent the day, taking it for granted that she should have first turn in the shower. Jill sank to a seat on the veranda and grimaced good-naturedly at her brother.

'It's a grand life if you don't weaken! I'm not at all sure that I wouldn't rather see my wild life behind bars after all. At least it doesn't take as long.'

'You're only moaning because I dragged you away from your new friend at the Lodge,' he came back. 'That was quite a line he was giving you when I came over.'

She giggled. 'Your French must be better than mine. I only understood about a quarter of what he was saying.'

'You didn't need any particular grasp of the language to get the message *he* was putting across. I got the distinct impression that I was anything but a welcome sight. Do you usually go around letting yourself be picked up that way?'

'Certainly not,' she came back demurely. 'Only when I know big brother is standing by ready to rescue me from a fate worse than death. Anyway, Henri was due to leave in the morning. I did understand that much. It's rather a quick turn-over they have in these parts, isn't it?'

'Fairly.' He was smiling. 'Fancying your chances with the next batch?'

'It all depends. How about it, Sara? Two would be safer than one. We could become the Belles of the Backwoods with little or no effort.'

Blue eyes met cool grey ones briefly. 'Sara isn't interested in boys,' said Steve.

'I'm not interested in boys either. Nothing under twenty-three, thanks!'

'What's your upper limit?' asked Don lazily, and Jill gave him a swift glance, her expression undergoing a slight, indecipherable change.

'I haven't thought about it. Should I have one?'

'Just to keep the record straight.'

Ted came up the steps from the compound to join them. 'Hi,' he said. 'Had a good day?'

'Reasonable,' answered Steve. 'Anything happened round here?'

'One of the boys got himself gored in the leg by a warthog. Nothing we can't handle right here. Apart from that it's been pretty quiet.' He made to move into the house to fix himself a drink, paused in the doorway and added, 'Nearly forgot the most important thing. Mgari sent a messenger across inviting all of us to a *ngoma* tonight.'

Sara looked up quickly. 'In aid of what?'

'He didn't say. There doesn't have to be any particular reason for a celebration. You know that. It might even be in honour of our visitors here,' with a grin which encompassed both Jill and Don. 'We'll find out when we get there.'

Both of the latter were looking interested. 'A tribal dance?' asked Don. 'Do you think I might get some shots of it?'

'You'll have to ask permission first,' Steve replied. 'These are very private affairs. It's a great honour to be invited at all.' His gaze rested on Sara. 'You know Mgari better than I do. How do you think he'll react to a camera?'

'It depends on what they're celebrating,' she answered steadily. 'I didn't realize you'd *met* Mgari.'

'I called in a week or so ago to introduce myself. He was most courteous, but rather more interested in the whereabouts of the *kidoga memsahib*.' There was a glint in the grey eyes. 'You seem to have created quite an impression.'

Sara gave him a bland little smile. 'He's a very discerning man – and he has a great regard for my father. This won't be the first *ngoma* I've been to, though it could probably be the last. Kimani said that he thought they would be moving on before long.'

'He's probably right. They're having to take the herds farther out each day to find good pasturage.' Steve straightened away from the rail. 'A few things I want to see to before I report in.'

He dropped laconically down the steps and strode off, a tall lean figure in bush shirt and shorts, bareheaded in the slanting afternoon sun.

'What time will we be due at this jamboree?' queried Don into the sudden small silence.

'Oh, we'll probably wander along about nine after we've eaten – unless you fancy a feast of cow's blood and milk?'

'Ugh!' Jill wrinkled her nose in disgust. 'I hope you're joking.'

'Not at all. The Masai don't normally eat meat. Actually, it's not at all bad.'

The other's eyes widened. 'You mean you've tried it?'

'Only once, when the tribe came here. Dad said it was a simple act of courtesy.'

'Rather you than me.' A change came over the vivacious face. 'You don't think we'll be expected to sample the stuff too, do you?'

'Well . . .' Sara replied gravely . . . 'if you're offered some it would be considered most impolite to refuse.'

'Then I don't think I can go. I just couldn't!'

'She's teasing you,' said Don on a lazy note of amusement.

'Are you?' Jill demanded, and Sara laughed.

'Just a little. Mgari is well aware that the European

diet is quite different. I shouldn't worry too much. All you'll have to do is sit there and watch their dancing and look as if you're enjoying it.' She paused. 'Perhaps someone ought to warn Diane to wear trousers. We'll be sitting on the floor on mats, and there are almost sure to be ants around.'

Jill got up. 'I'll go and tell her. She'll not want to be changing again after dinner.'

Ted was standing in the main doorway listening to the conversation with a grin on his lined features. He stood back to let Jill pass him, then slid into the seat she had vacated as though it had been too much trouble to walk the few steps to another.

'Talking of ants,' he said, 'did I ever tell you about that time we pitched camp right across the path of a column of soldiers?' He didn't bother to wait for Sara's reply. 'Two o'clock in the morning it was when they started coming through, and five near enough before they passed. Like a black tide, in at one tent flap and out at the other with me lying right there on the bed watching 'em and hoping like fury that none of 'em took a notion to shin up the legs.'

'I thought soldier ants ate everything in their path?' Don commented dryly. 'I read a tale once where they stripped a sleeping man to a skeleton.'

'Must have been tied down or dead drunk,' was the prompt reply. 'You don't lie quiet with those fellers on you. Only thing to do is get your clothes off and head for the nearest water. Mind you, there's still the hippos and crocs to think about.'

'It beats me how you ever came out of it all alive,' said Sara. 'Why don't you tell Don about the time you wrestled a lion?'

Ted grinned. 'I save that one for wide-eyed young-sters fresh out from town.' He caught the cushion she flung at him and tucked it comfortably behind his head. 'Before I forget, there's a letter for you from Dave. I put it in your room.'

'Why didn't you say!' She leaped to her feet, her smile bright. 'I never expected another so soon.'

Steve was coming in from the rear veranda as she went through to the corridor. His hair was damp and he had a towel in his hand. Sara steeled herself and ran a wide, admiring eye over his crisp slacks and shirt.

'Things to do, did you say? Stealing a march on the rest of us would be more like it. I'm sure Mgari will be flattered by so much preparation.'

His smile was sardonic. 'Nice to have you back to normal. I was getting quite worried.'

'Oh, you don't have to worry about me at any time.' Sara was amazed at her own lightness of tone. 'I'm inoculated against practically everything.'

'I hope so,' he said on an odd note, and went into his own room closing the door firmly between them.

The letter had been written in Benston where her father was staying with the old friends he had spoken of. Everything was just as he had left it, he said with enthusiasm. The church, the cottages down by the river; even the swans were still there. Nothing at all had changed. He kept repeating that as if he could scarcely believe it. The people he was staying with were a brother and sister he had grown up with right there in Benston. Sara wouldn't remember them, of course, al-though she had met them several times as a child.

Molly had been married herself then, but her husband had died six years ago and she had gone back to keep house for her brother who was a farmer. *Always was self-sacrificing,* he had written. *A woman like that deserves more out of life than she's had so far. You'd like her, Sara.*

Sara read and re-read that last paragraph, a faint frown touching her forehead. Dave should have got married again, Ted had said a few weeks back, and he was her father's closest friend. Was it possible that he recognized a need she hadn't seen herself? She and Dad had been so happy together this last three years, but a daughter was hardly the same as a wife in companionship. And this letter; the way he spoke of the woman he had known so well as a boy. If he did marry again what would she, Sara, do? She wouldn't be needed any more. There was an awful desolation in that thought.

The *ngoma* was already in full swing by the time they all arrived at the *boma*. Mgari greeted them cordially, and seated them on the rush matting along with himself and the other elders of the village, Sara on one side and Steve on his other. The dancing was non-stop; as one section of the community tired so another would leap to their feet and take their places, sometimes the women, sometimes the men, occasionally all together. Their vitality was electric, eyes flashing, teeth gleaming, bodies performing endless variations of movement to the rhythm of the drums. On several occasions the dancers stooped and gathered up handfuls of earth which they then allowed to trickle back through their fingers in a sifting motion.

'What's it all about?' asked Don *sotto voce* from his seat at Sara's side when an hour had passed. 'And how the devil long does it go on for?'

'They're praying for fertility,' she replied in the same low tones. She caught his quick sideways look and grinned. 'Of the earth. Good grazing for their cattle for the coming season. It goes on for hours, but we don't have to stay much longer. The thing was to put in an appearance after being specially invited.'

'Then if I'm going to get some film I ought to get started. Can you ask the old boy about it?'

Sara hesitated a moment before turning reluctantly towards Mgari and putting her request, indicating Don and his camera with a gesture of her hand. There was a second or two when she thought he was going to refuse, then he consulted briefly with the others nearby and finally gave permission.

Don already had his camera set up for night filming, and shot against the glow from the fires, moving round the dancers for several minutes. He came back looking pleased with himself, but didn't forget to say an *Asante* to Mgari for the privilege.

They left not long afterwards after prolonged farewells had taken place at the gateway to the *boma*. As on the outward journey, Diane took it for granted that she should sit up front with Steve, leaving the rest of them to pile into the back. Squashed up against Don on one side seat with Jill and Ted opposite, Sara tried not to watch the two up front, or listen to the lighthearted, slightly dangerous conversation taking place between them. They were both of them adept at carrying on *that* kind of affair. Sara couldn't imagine Diane becoming flustered by anything Steve might say to her.

She was last out of the car when they reached the Station, loitering deliberately until Jill had gone on ahead into the house with Ted.

'I must make sure that Kiki is all right in that cage before I go in,' she announced. 'Coming to keep me company, Don?' She had the satisfaction of seeing Steve look round as she slid a hand through the former's arm. 'You never know, I might find myself in need of protection.'

'First time I've ever been called on to play that role,' grinned Don, readily accompanying her towards the pens. 'Why have you got the monkey in a cage?'

'Because it's the only way to keep him out of the house while your sister is here,' she replied a trifle shortly, removing the hand from his sleeve once they were out of sight of the veranda. 'He isn't used to being locked up.'

'Well, it won't be for much longer,' he rejoined equably. 'Di can't help being the way she is about the creatures.'

'I know.' Sara was sorry for her spiteful little outburst. 'And it won't really do him any harm for a few days. I was just being bitchy.'

Don laughed. 'And refreshingly honest about it! I've never met a girl quite like you before, Sara Macdonald.'

She gave him a mischievous sideways glance. 'Someone else said that to me not so long ago.'

'Another man?'

'Almost. A very nice boy, at any rate. He wanted me to visit him in the States.'

'And are you going to?'

'I might do some day. I might do all sorts of things some day.' Her tone altered a little. 'According to some people I've missed *such* a lot living in the jungle these last three years. Do you think I'm backward, Don?'

'I think you're a tantalizing little witch,' he said with deliberation. 'And you're not getting away with it.' He took her by the shoulders and turned her towards him, smiling down at her in the darkness. 'The monkey can wait a couple more minutes, can't it?'

'If he has to.' Sara hesitated, added in low tones, 'Don, I'd rather you didn't. I – I don't feel like being kissed at the moment. I'm not being coy, or anything like that, honestly. It's just that I . . .'

'It's just that you're not sure yet whether you like me that way or not.' His shrug was easy. 'Okay, I won't push it. Only don't try flirting if you're not willing to follow through. Next time you might not find me in as passive a mood!'

'I won't,' she promised, and added impulsively, 'You are nice, Don!'

'Another first!' His tone was dryly humorous. 'I'll have to be looking out my halo. Come on, let's get these animals seen to and make tracks for the house while my resolution holds out.'

Steve was waiting at the top of the veranda steps when they reached the house again. 'Everything all right?' he asked Sara pointedly.

She gave him an unblinking stare. 'Everything is fine. You didn't have to wait up.'

'I didn't,' he returned. 'I have a report to write before I turn in. Good night.'

They both replied in unison, passing him and going indoors together to part in the corridor and go their separate ways.

Jill was still asleep when Sara got up at six. When she got outside, Steve was leaning on the rail just as she had last seen him, except that he was back in working gear. He greeted her without expression.

'Jill not awake yet?' he asked.

'No.' She hesitated, wanting to go and stay both at the same time. 'I'm going up to the bluff.'

'I know.' He glanced up at the rocky face outlined against the paling sky. 'You spend a lot of time up there.'

'Yes,' she said again.

He stirred suddenly. 'Mind if I come with you?'

Sara didn't turn her head, afraid of revealing too much. 'I don't suppose I could really stop you,' she said, and then flushed because she hadn't meant to sound quite so ungracious. 'No, I don't mind,' she tagged on quickly. 'Please do.'

She was very conscious of his height and lean strength as they moved through the low bush to the foot of the bluff, and was grateful when he made no attempt to lend her a helping hand as Travis had done. He was right behind her when they reached her usual spot. He leaned against the rock face to scan the emerging landscape, his hand reaching automatically for the pack of cigarettes.

'You smoke too much,' Sara observed without thinking, and could have bitten out her tongue as he gave her an amused glance.

'You sound like Jill. Does my health concern

you?'

'Not unduly,' she came back on a reasonably light note. 'I'm just a born nosy-parker. What do you think?' with a sweep of her hand which indicated the distances about them.

'Pretty good vantage point. I can see why you like coming up here – particularly at this hour.' He paused. 'You'd miss it, wouldn't you, all this?'

'Yes,' she answered softly, 'I would.'

'But you can't expect to spend the rest of your life here. Some day you're going to meet someone you'll want to marry, and he won't necessarily be content to stay here.'

A sudden huskiness in her voice, she said, 'Why is it that the female is supposed to make all the sacrifices?'

'Because man is the provider and he's entitled to choose where he'll live and work.'

'Even if his wife is unhappy there?'

His mouth twisted slightly. 'If she thought enough about him it wouldn't make any difference. A woman should be ready to follow her man to the end of the earth if necessary.'

Was he thinking of Diane? Sara wondered. Had she already made it plain to him that a few days of back-wood living were as much as she was prepared to stand? Perhaps the whole idea of buying the adjoining farm was an effort at compromise, a means of having the woman he wanted while still retaining some measure of independence. Yet she wouldn't have thought Steve a man to settle for compromise under any circumstances. Or was it simply that she didn't want to think of him that way because of the implications? Sara became aware of a tight dryness in her throat, and hastily shied away from further introspection.

There was a silence between them for the space of several minutes. Steve finished the cigarette and stubbed it out, resettled himself against the rock and said evenly, 'You know about Don's wife, I suppose?'

She glanced at him quickly and away again. 'I know he's been married, yes.'

His eyes were narrowed against the growing brightness of the eastern skyline. 'Are you attracted to him?'

'He's a very attractive man,' she answered at last, and then with a touch of asperity, 'I'm old enough to recognize that much.'

'I wouldn't argue with it.' His glance slid over her small, fine features. 'All the same, I wouldn't pay too much attention to anything he might say to you. Don's okay in his way, but he's not concerned with finer feelings.'

'Not to be trusted is what you're really saying,' she rejoined on a brittle note. 'Do you think you know him all that well?'

'Better than you do. I'm trying to be diplomatic about this, so stop jumping down my throat before I've finished. Don laid the blame for the breakdown of his marriage entirely at his wife's door, and even if he doesn't fully appreciate the fact himself, he's intent on taking it out on every other female. I wouldn't like to see you get hurt.'

Her head came up. 'I shan't get hurt by anyone.

Odd as it might seem to you, I can appreciate that a kiss or so doesn't have to mean anything.'

'Then he has kissed you?' he said sharply.

Sara bit her lip, but pride wouldn't let her back out now. 'Why shouldn't he? You did.'

His mouth twisted. 'I hadn't forgotten. There's a difference between my intentions and his.'

'You don't need to tell me that,' she retorted. 'There's a world of difference between *you* and Don. You might try finding out the real reason his wife left him before slinging any more mud around, for instance!'

He studied her, his jaw hard. 'Supposing you tell me.'

'It isn't up to me.' She was already regretting the hastily spoken words. 'Ask someone closer to him.'

'Meaning Diane, I imagine. Is she supposed to have had something to do with it?'

Sara moved abruptly. This whole matter had gone far enough. They had no right to be standing here discussing Don's affairs. 'I'm going down,' she said.

'No, you're not.' He hadn't moved himself, but there was a look in his eyes which dared her to try passing him. 'I want to know what you were getting at.'

'Then you'll have to want.'

A muscle tautened in his cheek. 'I've never known anyone go out of their way to beg for trouble like you do. Maybe it's a good thing the Milsons aren't going to be here more than a few days. It would be like you to deliberately encourage Don just to get back at me.'

Trembling but controlling her voice, Sara said, 'Don't flatter yourself. If I encourage Don at all it's because it happens to be a refreshing change to be credited with a little intelligence!' That was unfair and she knew it, but she was beyond caring about shades of meaning. 'Ever since you arrived at Kambala you've acted as if no one else knew anything at all about the job ... including my father! You started throwing your weight around that first day, and you haven't stopped since! You even had to ruin this place for me!'

'Finished?' he inquired stonily into the sudden silence. 'Since we seem to be exchanging a few home truths this morning let's expound on a couple. I've never met your father, but any man who can just take off for England and leave his daughter alone in a place as remote as this doesn't in my view show any sense of responsibility.'

'He didn't leave me alone,' she protested. 'There was Ted and Kimani.'

'Neither of whom were in any position to enforce any control over your movements, it seems.'

'That's not what you said to Ted the day I cracked the axle.'

'I know that's not what I said to Ted. I was ready to let fly at anybody right then. I was sent out here to do a specific job, not play nursemaid to another man's responsibility. If you'd been reasonable from the start we'd have got along okay, but you're still about as easy to handle as a porcupine!' His voice had a vicious edge. 'When are you going to learn the difference between officiousness and common sense?'

Common sense, thought Sara numbly, seemed to have little to do with anything right at the moment.

She said thickly, 'Are you so sure you know it yourself? Perhaps it would be good for me to fall in love with Don, even if it was only to teach me that lesson you seem to think I need. On the other hand, I might turn out to be just what *he* needs!'

'That I don't doubt. Some men get a real kick out of teaching a young innocent the facts of life.' His mouth was a hard straight line. 'Luckily he won't get the chance. If necessary I'll have a word with him myself.'

Her face went hot. 'You have no right to do that! This hardly comes under station regulations. In any case, what makes you think that Don would take any notice of what you say?'

'If he doesn't he'll be out of here quicker than he expects.' He studied her grimly. 'The choice is yours. Either you discourage him yourself or I do it for you. Which?'

The whole situation had grown out of proportion, but this was no time to be arguing that point. Steve was perfectly capable of doing as he said, and if he did Don could only think that she herself had taken things a little too seriously and gone to him for advice. Hands clenched moistly at her sides, she said tautly, 'That isn't a choice, it's an ultimatum.'

He shrugged. 'Have it your own way.'

'No.' She swallowed. 'Leave Don out of it. I won't let him near me again. Now do you mind if we go back?'

'We'll both go back,' he said coolly.

Njorogi was setting the table along the veranda when they reached the house. He gave them both a cheerful greeting and went on methodically with his task, wiping out each cup with a clean cloth before setting it carefully upside down in its saucer. Steve disappeared round the back, leaving Sara to sink into a chair and wish suddenly and desperately that she had accompanied her father to England after all.

# CHAPTER SIX

IT was a quiet week-end. After two days of bumping around in the Land Rover, both the Milsons and Jill seemed content to spend their time just lounging around the house and veranda. Apart from one brief sortie on the Sunday morning, Steve stayed on the station too, suggesting to Sara that he didn't trust her to keep her word and meant to ensure her adherence to his instructions by keeping an eye on Don himself. Under his watchful gaze she felt self-conscious and uncomfortable with the former, and knew that Don was puzzled by the change in her. She would be more than relieved when it came to the time for the Milsons to depart, she decided.

There was a storm on the Sunday evening, starting before dinner and continuing on through the meal in a steady roar of rain and rolling thunder which died away gradually to the north. After it the air had cooled far too much to allow sitting on the veranda with their coffee, so they dispersed themselves about the living-room.

Sitting on one of the rugs with her head back against the arm of Ted's chair, Sara tried not to notice how close Diane was to Steve on the settee, how her amber-tipped fingers rested lightly and intimately on his arm as she leaned over to put her cup down on the table close to his knee. Everything the older woman did was somehow calculated, she thought, and immediately took herself to task for a cattiness hitherto quite foreign to her make-up. Diane had never been anything but pleasant to her.

Jill seemed restless after the storm had passed, wandering from window to window, in between fingering disinterestedly through the pile of old magazines. Eventually, as if able to stand inaction any longer, she got up and put a record on the ancient turntable, wound the handle and stood listening to the scratchy music for a brief moment before turning to look at Don with a sudden brilliant smile.

'Dance with me,' she invited. 'I'll go mad if I sit around much longer.'

Don smiled back and rose to oblige. They moved slowly around the clear space of floor in the middle of the room, a tall, indolently good-looking man and a vivaciously lovely girl who looked as if they had danced together many times before. Yet Jill couldn't have known Don more than three weeks at the outside, Sara reckoned. Her thoughts harkened back to the first evening they had all arrived at Kambala when Don had walked her down to the orphanage, and his comments on Jill's probable reactions to the quieter life on the station. She hadn't thought anything about it at the time, but now it came to her that Don had seemed to know rather a lot about Jill under the circumstances. Glancing at Steve, she saw that he too was watching the gyrating couple with slightly narrowed eyes. Obviously it had not occurred to him that his own sister might be in danger of becoming involved with the handsome Don, perhaps because he had credited her with rather more sense. Sara wondered how he would handle this new situation, whether he would tackle Jill on the subject in the same way he had tackled her the morning before. Somehow she doubted it. With someone he cared about rather than merely felt responsible for it would be kid gloves over the iron hand.

The music came to an eventual stop, and Jill disengaged herself from Don's arms to go and put on another record. He immediately came over to where Sara sat and pulled her to her feet, shrugging aside her protestations that she couldn't dance properly with the assurance that she would find it easy enough to follow him once they got started. As it turned out, Sara did, but she was uncomfortably aware of everyone's eyes on the two of them, of Jill's stiff little smile as she stood by the record player and Steve's total lack of expression. She was glad when the record ran down in the middle of the number, giving her an excuse to make her escape.

'Not at all bad for a beginner,' commented Diane lightly. 'With a little practice you'd be as good a dancer as anyone I know. It's a pity you're so far away from any kind of entertainment out here. You'll have to come and stay with us some time and let us show you how the rest of the world lives.' She paused as if a thought had just occurred to her. 'In fact, why not come back with us on Tuesday? Your father is due home in about three weeks, isn't he?'

'Yes,' Sara acknowledged, 'but . . .'

'Well then, you'd be in Nairobi to meet his plane, and you could have a good time until then. I'm sure Jill would be pleased to have someone her own age in the house for a week or two until Steve gets back to finish his leave.'

A small silence descended over the room. Jill had flushed and Steve was sitting up suddenly straighter, his gaze on his sister's face.

'Jill?' he demanded.

Diane looked from one to the other of them and her expression altered. 'You mean you haven't told him yet?'

'Told me what?' Steve's voice was quiet but edged. 'I was under the impression that you were staying on for a week or two, Jill.'

'I was.' She hesitated, then shrugged with a wry little smile. 'I just didn't realize how ... deadly dull it was going to be. Sara's all right because she's used to it, but I ... well, I'd go crackers if I had to spend every day and night doing the same old things. I'm sorry, Steve, really I am. You know there's nothing I like better than to see you.'

'But not at the cost of your personal enjoyment,' he said dryly. 'All right, it's understandable. I should have thought about it before.' His glance moved to Sara. 'Well, what about it?'

She hardly knew what to say, or even what she wanted to say. Steve might have reservations about her association with Don here on Kambala, but it was certain that he had even more over Jill's feelings for the man away from here. If Don's game was to play one girl off against another, as he appeared to have been doing tonight, then her own presence in the Milson household would hardly command Jill's friendship. Yet if she didn't go there was a chance that he might take rather more advantage of Jill's obvious attraction to him than she perhaps bargained for. On her arrival Sara had thought the other girl sophisticated and knowledgeable in a way she could never be. Now, after seeing her almost beg Don to take notice of her, she wasn't so sure. As for Don himself, her opinion of him had undergone an abrupt volte-face after the deliberate way in which he had left Jill standing. It seemed that Steve might even be right about him. He did like to hurt.

The whole room seemed to be waiting for her answer. She said slowly, 'I haven't got the clothes for visiting, I'm afraid.'

'You could kit yourself out while you're down there,' put in Ted, speaking for the first time in about twenty minutes. 'You've never touched that account Dave opened for you at the bank the last time you were in Nairobi. And you could visit Kimani. He's going to be in hospital for some time with that fractured thigh, according to reports.'

That appeared to settle it. Sara looked across at Diane and tried to sound suitably pleased about it. 'It's very good of you to ask me. Thank you.'

'Then that's settled.' There was a note of satisfaction in her voice. 'You'll have to let me show you the best places to shop. Not that there's any need to buy so much, apart from a few dresses suitable for back here too.' For a moment her eyes met Steve's, and she smiled with a hint of intimacy. 'And in three weeks we'll expect you back in town yourself.'

'I'll be there.' It was said with assurance. He got abruptly to his feet. 'Anyone for a drink?'

By Monday night Sara had reached a fatalistic state of acceptance over the coming visit. She didn't want to go and it was no use pretending that she did, but it was too late to back out of it now.

Since Sunday she had battled silently with the suspicion that it was Steve she regretted leaving even more than Kambala itself – battled and lost. Their relationship had been brief, tempestuous and in many ways enraging, but her whole life had changed on the day he had arrived here. Not that acknowledging his attraction for her was going to do her any good. He still saw her as a troublesome youngster, and was hardly likely to miss her, she told herself bleakly. Diane was the kind of woman he wanted. Diane was the kind of woman any man would want.

She was still awake at three when she heard Steve's door open and close softly. Without thinking about it, she slid quietly out of the narrow bed and opened her own door, standing there for a moment listening. There was a clink of glass from the direction of the living-room, although no light showed. Recalling that other night when he had been out chasing the poachers, Sara crept along the corridor and gently eased open the door, no clear idea in her mind. Unable to see anyone in the vicinity of the drinks cabinet, she pushed the door a little wider, and almost fell into the room as he spoke.

'Curiosity killed the cat – or are you walking in your sleep?'

He was sitting in a chair beyond the doorway. Sara had a feeling that he had known she would follow him and had seated himself there deliberately to wait for her. She was glad of the darkness at that moment. If she couldn't see his face properly it was unlikely that he could see hers either. The knowledge gave her confidence.

'I heard a noise,' she said. 'I didn't know it was you.'

'Who were you hoping for?'

It was a moment before she answered that one. 'Ted sometimes wanders about in the middle of the night.'

'As well? We seem to be a household of insomniacs.' There was a pause, then he added in a slightly different tone, 'I'd advise a wrap of some kind if you plan to do any night-prowling while you're with the Milsons. You're liable to catch a chill like that.'

'I'm not cold,' she denied. 'And I don't have a wrap. In any case, I'm . . .'

'In any case . . . what?' he prompted as she paused.

'Nothing.' She half turned back the way she had come. 'I'm sorry if I disturbed you.'

'You've done little else but since I got here,' he said dryly. 'Looking forward to tomorrow's trip?'

'I suppose so.' She hovered uncertainly, trying to gauge his mood. 'At least I won't be bothering you any more.'

'No.' His tone was enigmatic. 'Quite a relief. By the time we meet again you might have stopped disliking me quite so much.'

Her breath caught. 'I . . . don't dislike you,' she managed.

'You've given a very good impression of it at times.'

'If I have it's because you've provoked me into it.'

'Is that so?' He considered her with his head on one side, then his mouth lifted suddenly and unexpectedly into a smile. 'Maybe you're right at that. There's something about you that would provoke any man into asserting himself. You're too damned independent, for one thing. You'd get a lot further if you learned to lean a little.'

There was a fascination in speaking with Steve like this. Sara felt her own mouth curving in response. 'On you?' she asked. 'It's a bit late for that now.'

'It's never too late.' His voice changed again subtly. 'Sara, I want you to promise me something.'

She stiffened. 'What?'

'That you won't let Don come between you and Jill. The two of you were getting along fine until Sunday night. Since then you've barely spoken a word to each other. He's not worth it.'

'Have you told Jill that too?'

'It wouldn't be much use telling Jill anything right now. She's infatuated with him and hardly likely to listen to anything against him.'

'It's only a couple of days ago that you were classing me in the same state of mind,' she pointed out. 'I don't seem to remember you pulling any punches *that* time!'

'You're a different proposition. You don't respond to gentle handling. Basically, I think you probably saw through Don from the start, only you liked the attention he paid you too much to listen to instinct.' He leaned forward in his chair, resting his elbows on his knees with the glass between his hands. 'I'm asking for your help, Sara.'

She was silent for a long moment. 'The way I see it,' she said at last, 'is that you want me to try to persuade Jill that Don is no good by treating him with contempt myself.'

'Something like that.'

'Why don't you try telling him to leave her alone? Or better still, why not simply send her back to Mombasa where he won't be able to get to her?'

He made a shrugging movement. 'Because neither course would work. I want Jill to get over it herself, and the quickest way she's going to do that is by seeing him for what he is.'

'Supposing he were really in love with her, and she with him?' Sara suggested unsteadily. 'Would you still be against him?'

His head lifted. 'For Jill, yes. He's too old for her, for one thing.'

A tightness came into her chest. 'I don't see why that should have anything to do with it.'

'Well, it does,' he retorted roughly. 'Anyway, the question doesn't arise. Stop prevaricating, Sara. You assessed Don pretty thoroughly on Sunday night, and you can open Jill's eyes to him too if you really put your mind to it. The question is, will you?'

'I can try,' she said at last. 'Only don't blame me if I fail to get through. Jill is too much like you to take kindly to my interference.'

Steve's mouth quirked suddenly. 'Just can't resist a dig, can you? You'd be surprised how much leeway I've allowed you this last few weeks.'

The familiar irritation swamped all other sensations. 'If I'm old enough to be entrusted with this little job than I'm old enough to be regarded as an adult now, so stop patronizing me, will you? I'm sick of it!' She half turned to make for the door, barked her shin violently against the sharp edge of a stool and gave an involuntary exclamation of pain.

Steve was on his feet and beside her before she could move, swinging her up in his arms to carry her back to the chair he had just vacated and deposited her there. Kneeling in front of her, he rubbed the injured spot gently through the thin cotton of her pyjamas with the palm of his hand for a moment, then sat back on his heels to look at her with a faintly twisted smile.

'You're a fireball, Sara Macdonald. You should carry a warning: light the blue touch paper and stand well clear! Is the pain going off?'

Having him there in front of her like this gave her a sensation which was pain and pleasure combined. She had to fight against the sudden desperate urge to put out her hand and touch her fingers to the strong mouth.

'I think I'd better go back to bed,' she said huskily. 'I . . . It's going to be a long day.'

It was a moment before he moved, then abruptly he stood up. 'It would seem to be a good idea. And don't forget what we talked about.'

'I won't.' She was on her feet, suddenly desperate to get away from him. 'Good night, Steve.'

'Sleep tight.' There was an edge of irony to his voice. As she moved towards the door he picked up the discarded glass and lifted it to his lips with an air of having already dismissed her from his mind.

# CHAPTER SEVEN

THE Milson farm was some ten miles out of Nairobi
at the foot of the Ngong Hills, the house Spanish style
and impressive. Familiar with the shabby homeliness
of the *banda* at Kambala, Sara found the whole place
rather overpowering in its luxurious appointments and
superbly tiled floors. Obviously the Milsons were not
reliant solely on the income derived from running the
farm itself, which explained how it was that both of
them could afford the time to make trips like the one
from which they had just returned.

She met and liked Barry Seymour, Don's manager,
who had been left in charge during the last week, and
was not slow to note the way in which the younger
man's eyes followed Jill everywhere, although the
latter appeared quite unaware of it herself.

Nairobi was chock-a-block with tourists, the wide
main streets packed with cars. Under Diane and Jill's
direction, Sara brought three cotton dresses for day
wear, and a long one in varying shades of blue with a
scooped neckline and tiny sleeves which fitted her like a
glove – necessary, as Diane remarked, if they were to
visit the country club while she was with them. For the
rest, she was already in possession of several pairs of
perfectly wearable trousers, she declared, and stead-
fastly refused to spend any more on clothes she would
hardly be needing back at Kambala.

She managed to get to see Kimani in hospital,

finding him resigned to a stay of a week or two if not exactly happy about it. The break had been a bad one, and his leg was in traction. He too doubted very much that he would be returning to Mara at all in the foreseeable future. Sara left with the assurance that she would call in again before she went back herself.

It was Jill who made the tentative suggestion that she should have something done about her hair. It was such an unusual colour, she said, it seemed a shame not to have it properly shaped while she had the opportunity. Sara accepted the overture in the spirit in which it was offered, and accompanied Steve's sister to an appointment at Schoutens, emerging somewhat self-consciously an hour later with a sleek, head-hugging cut which subtly altered the shaping of her face and raised Don's eyebrows in approval when he saw her on their return to the house.

'Amazing what a little polish can do,' he commented. 'Now we must arrange the ball.'

'You make a lousy fairy godmother,' said his sister dryly. 'How about the club? Jill's been before, of course, but you'll find everybody friendly enough down there, Sara.' Her tone was faintly disparaging. 'Don can squire the two of you. I have other things to do this week-end.'

Sara said quickly, 'What about Barry? He could make it a foursome.'

'Barry?' Don sounded momentarily taken aback. 'Well, yes, I suppose he could.' Her glance at her brother held an element of irony. 'It would take the strain off you.'

'It's fine by me,' was the equable reply. 'I'll suggest it

to him this afternoon – unless Jill would prefer to do it for me?'

'It's hardly my place.' Jill's voice had a barely perceptible quiver. 'I think I'll have a lie down before lunch. It was dreadfully hot in the car.'

There was a brief pause after she had left the room. Diane was the first to move. 'I've a few things to do myself,' she murmured, and sauntered out, leaving Sara and Don alone.

'Why Barry?' asked the latter without preamble.

Sara gave him a direct look. 'Why not? I thought he seemed rather nice.'

'It's Jill he's interested in.'

'I know. That's why I suggested him.'

His smile was unexpected. 'Quite the little matchmaker, aren't you? What makes you think that your ruse is going to make any difference to the way Jill feels about me?'

'It's just possible that she might appreciate the differences between you,' Sara retorted promptly. 'At least Barry isn't out to make a fool of her.'

'And I am?' He looked interested. 'You've obviously been doing some research into the subject. What farseeing conclusions have you reached?'

'Nothing you don't know about yourself already. You encouraged Jill to fall for you to satisfy your own ego, then got bored with her when she started to make it too obvious how she felt.'

'Is that your version or hers?'

'Mine, of course. Jill hasn't discussed you with me at any time – apart from that first afternoon when she told me you'd been married.'

141

'Then you want to get your facts straight. Jill is a pretty girl and I enjoyed taking her around during those weeks after Steve left, but I never gave her any cause to think that I might be getting any serious thoughts about us.'

'You must have kissed her.'

'Naturally. She expected it. She even asked for it – like someone else I could mention.'

Sara flushed. 'That was different.'

'I know.' His light blue eyes were shrewd. 'You were using me to try to make Steve jealous. Did you think I wasn't aware of it? I'm not sure exactly how far things had gone between you two when we arrived and broke it up, but I could see how you felt about him from the first. You used me, so I used you. I thought that if I paid you enough attention Jill might get the point. Trouble is that I found myself getting too interested in you. You're quite a girl, Sara.'

She was totally nonplussed, hardly knowing whether to believe him or not. Yet everything he had said rang true. It was only Steve's summing up of him which had changed her original assessment and made her suspicious of his motives.

'So what happens now?' she asked after a long pause.

'That's rather up to you. It would be simple enough to carry on in the same way from my point of view.'

Sara looked at him uncertainly. 'You mean to pretend to an interest in each other so that Jill will be put off?'

'Except that on my side it wouldn't be all pretence. Not that you have to worry,' he added on a smile. 'I wouldn't take advantage of it.'

It was ironical, she thought, that the obvious solution should lie so directly at odds with what Steve had asked of her. 'I don't want to fall out with Jill,' she said slowly.

'I don't think that will happen. Jill is basically a nice girl. She won't hold it against you that I'm attracted to you. She may be hurt at first, but it won't last. She was ready to fall for somebody when she first came up here, and I happened to be the one she chose. It could have been Barry, or any one of half a dozen others, only she didn't see as much of them. Propinquity can have quite an effect on the emotions.'

Sara looked back at him steadily. 'Are you trying to tell me something?'

'I suppose what I'm trying to say is that your feelings for Steve are probably about the same as Jill's for me, except that I'm not sure how he would have handled his side of it. The point is that now you're away from him you stand a better chance of getting over it quickly, especially as you must have realized how things are between him and Diane.'

A shutter came down over her emotions. Don would possibly believe her if she denied that there had been anything at all between her and Steve, but it wouldn't make any difference at all to the situation as it stood. Maybe he was even right about distance lending a certain disenchantment.

'All right,' she said. 'I think you might have given Jill a bit more encouragement than you say you did, but that's immaterial now. Are you going to tell Diane about all this?'

'What for? She's only concerned with her own affairs.' His tone was matter-of-fact. 'This will be just between the two of us. That's best.'

It might be best from Don's point of view, but it left Sara with an uneasy feeling that she was going to regret this whole arrangement some time in the not too distant future, although she couldn't at the moment have explained why.

The following week seemed one long round of festivities. Unaccustomed as she was to living it up, Sara found herself sometimes just a little overwhelmed by the bewildering variety of people, places and entertainments which came her way, yet at the same time enjoying it because it took her mind off other matters. She was also relieved to see Jill turning more and more to Barry as she came to accept the fact that Don wasn't for her, hiding her hurt behind a cheerful façade which faltered only on the rare occasions when she thought no one was observing her. Sara could sympathize with her. She had fallen, and fallen hard for a man who had seemed the epitome of everything wonderful, and the knowledge that one's idol apparently had feet of clay would be far from easy to accept.

So far as she herself was concerned, Don behaved himself with a decorum which both surprised and faintly piqued her. For a man who had professed an interest which had grown despite his inclinations his attitude was unusual, to say the least – more brotherly than lover-like. They went everywhere together, sometimes with Jill and Barry, often alone, yet so far he hadn't even attempted to kiss her.

Not that she wanted him to make love to her, she

told herself on the second Saturday evening as she once again made ready to visit the club. It was simply that she needed the reassurance of knowing that he still found her an attractive as well as a good companion. It was mainly for that reason, she admitted, that she had brought this other new dress, although it was a cause which should have put her to shame. Nevertheless, she was aware that she had never looked quite as she did at the moment, with her shoulders bared by the halter neckline and her hips slender beneath the softly flaring skirt in deep amber crepe which so enhanced her colouring. If Steve could see her now he wouldn't call her a kid, she thought, and squashed the sudden flare of longing before it could get properly started.

Diane had once again declined to attend the club that weekend, which left the four of them to pile into Don's car and drive there together. Sara had by now met most of the members, and felt almost familiar with her surroundings as she walked into the bar at Don's side with Jill and Barry a few paces behind. The knowledge that the dress was drawing considerable attention from both male and female eyes gave her a wholly new confidence. By the time Don took her onto the dance floor she felt she was walking on air.

'Enjoying yourself?' he asked softly, and she gave him a sparkling glance.

'Oh yes! Everyone is so nice.'

'Including me?'

She looked at him from beneath her lashes. 'Of course.'

'Then it's high time I changed my image. When a beautiful girl calls a man nice to his face it's death to the ego!'

'Am I?' she asked guilelessly. 'Beautiful, I mean.'

'You are now. You were only pretty before.'

'Before what?'

'Before you started realizing your potential,' he told her with deliberation. 'You've changed this last couple of weeks, Sara. Is it presumptuous of me to believe that I might have had something to do with it?'

Her smile was provocative. 'Not at all. If it wasn't for you and Diane I'd still be out at Kambala. You've both been very kind.'

'Nice, and now kind,' he growled in mock disgust. 'You need your ideas shaking up, young woman!'

'Oh?' She widened her eyes at him. 'When?'

His own eyes glinted suddenly. 'No time like the present. Let's go out on the terrace.'

Sara went unprotestingly, carried along on the crest of a wave she had no desire to stem. It was cool outside, and she gave a small involuntary shiver as they stood looking out over the lights of the city spreading away into the distance. Don drew her close, turning her in his arms to smile down into her upturned face. She met his kiss frankly and eagerly, sliding her arms up around his neck and feeling his tightening about her.

'So it did work,' he said softly when he eventually released her. 'It's been quite a strain stopping myself from doing that before, but my guess was right. You only want what you have to fight for, Sara Macdonald. That's why you wore that dress tonight, isn't it? To make me sit up and take notice.'

'Yes,' she admitted. She was aware of a vague sense of deflation she couldn't explain. She had wanted Don to kiss her, and had enjoyed it while it lasted, yet there seemed to be something missing now that it was over. She felt so cool and calm about it all, and she didn't want to feel that way. She wanted to be in love with Don in the same way she had thought herself in love with Steve, wildly, excitingly, even painfully. Yet what did she know about love? Perhaps this was the way the real kind came along; liking someone, enjoying his company as well as his embraces, building up gradually into the more passionate emotion. What she had felt for Steve had been simple schoolgirl infatuation, proven by the fact that she had got over him so quickly. All he had done was awaken her to the realization of needs other than the ones she was fulfilling out at Kambala, made her start to grow up. For that she supposed she should be grateful to him.

'Hey!' Don touched her lightly on the cheek. 'You've gone very quiet.' There was an unaccustomed note of uncertainty in his voice. 'Disappointed?'

'No.' She smiled at him brightly. 'How could any girl be disappointed in you, Don? You're the kind we all dream about. The dashing, handsome man of the world we're all supposed to have our sights set on getting.'

'Cynicism from you?' He was looking at her with an odd expression. 'Was that because you have doubts about what I am after myself?'

'Perhaps.' She half turned away from him. 'What *are* you after, Don?'

His hands were warm on her shoulders as he bent his head and touched his lips to her nape. 'I could say marriage, but it wouldn't be entirely true. Not yet. I'm not sure I could ever trust anyone that far again. Can we just leave it that you're the best thing that's happened to me in years for the present, and take it from there as it comes? Or is it too selfish of me to want to keep you to myself on those terms?'

'No,' she answered very softly. 'I think it's very honest of you, and good for us both.'

'Then that's how it will be.'

'My father will be back in just over a week,' she reminded him. 'You realize that I'll be going back to Kambala with him.'

'We'll talk about that when the time comes. A lot cal. happen in a week.' His smile was just faintly ironical. 'After all, you got over Steve York in less than that time.'

'Yes.' She paused. 'Don, there was never anything between Steve and me. It was all one-sided.'

'Oh?' He studied her. 'He never even kissed you?'

'Well . . . yes, he did. But . . .'

'Then it certainly wasn't entirely one-sided. Not that I blame him. I daresay I'd have found the temptation irresistible too.' He slid his arm further about her shoulders, turning her towards the doors. 'You're starting to feel chilly, and we'll have aroused enough speculation by coming out here alone in the first place. You realize you're associating with a man of somewhat doubtful principles, don't you?'

'They don't know you too well,' she responded. 'And I'm not in the least bit worried about what anyone in there might think.'

'Then you should be. It's different for a woman.'

'I don't see why it should be. People will think what

148

they want to think regardless of what we do or don't do.' Laughing, she put her arm through his as he pushed open the door. 'Is this circumspect enough?'

The group standing a few paces away looked round as one as they entered, and Sara felt the laughter die suddenly on her lips as her eyes met those of the tall man in the white dinner jacket whose mouth had taken on a hard line. Beside her she felt Don stiffen a little, then relax, heard his voice saying lightly, 'Quite a surprise, Steve. We weren't expecting you for another week or so.'

'No.' The reply was cool. 'Bruce Madden decided to relieve me. He thought the air up there might do him good after his spell in dock.'

'When did you get in?'

'About an hour or so ago.' It was Diane who answered for him, composed and striking in emerald green. Her hand was on Steve's arm possessively. 'We decided to come over and join the party. After all, it's Steve's first chance to see a bit of life in weeks.'

'For someone who only this afternoon condemned this whole place as a funeral parlour you changed your mind pretty quickly,' remarked her brother satirically, and received a totally unperturbed smile.

'It's the people who make a place, darling, as I'm sure you'll agree. We were wondering where you and Sara had got to.'

'We went out to get a breath of air,' put in Sara, feeling that it was time she said something.

'Without a wrap?' Steve's eyes slid over her bare shoulders, came back to her face and rested there inexorably. 'You're asking for a chill running around like that after dark. You should have more sense, Don.'

'I know. I realized that a moment ago.' Don looked down at her, mouth wry. 'How about a drink to chase away any goosepimples?'

'I . . .' she began, then she caught Steve's glance again and her chin lifted. 'A good idea,' she said brightly. 'Why don't we all have a drink to welcome Steve back to the civilized world?'

The six of them made quite a crowd in the bar. Sara sipped gingerly at the gin and orange she had asked for, finding the mix too strong for her taste yet reluctant to admit it with Steve watching her the way he was. She hardly knew whether to be relieved or sorry when he suggested that they go and dance, knowing full well what was coming once he got her alone.

He and Don were much of a height, she found, when they were on the floor; with both of them her eyes came exactly level with the second shirt button. But there the similarity ended. Whereas Don held her close with his breath stirring her hair, Steve's hands were hard at her back and there were several inches of space between them. His mouth was compressed, the grey eyes like granite.

'Quite a girl, aren't you?' he said. 'From duckling to swan all in a week!'

'Ten days, actually,' she murmured, and felt his fingers dig painfully into the centre of her back.

'Don't tempt providence. The way I feel at the moment I could do something drastic to you!'

Safe on a crowded dance floor, she dug up her most innocent smile. 'Would I enjoy it?'

He drew in a harsh breath. 'Cut it out. You might

have learned a great deal while you've been staying with the Milsons, but that dress doesn't make you too old to spank.'

'That would be a new kind of floor show.' Recklessly she went on, 'What do you think of my dress? Quite an improvement on trousers, don't you think?'

The music stopped. Steve took her firmly by the shoulders and pressed her ahead of him through the other dancers and out into the foyer, then from there to the door through which she and Don had entered a short time ago. The terrace was still empty. With the door closed behind him, Steve regarded her unsmilingly.

'Now try being funny.'

Recalling the last time he had cornered her like this, Sara thought that she had never felt less like being funny in her life. Yet she wasn't afraid of him – not unless fear came in different guises. What exactly her emotions did consist of at this moment she wasn't wholly certain. All she did know was that nothing had changed since she had last seen him, that he still looked on her as a bit of a kid he could bully around when he felt like it.

'I still don't have a wrap,' she pointed out coolly.

He took off his jacket and slung it about her shoulders, holding on to the lapels so that she was forced to face up to him. 'So now we get down to brass tacks,' he said grimly. 'Just what is going on between you and Don?'

She met his gaze stonily. 'Why don't you ask him?'

'I'm asking you!'

'Would you believe me if I told you nothing at all?'

'Would I hell!'

'Then I won't.' Despite herself she could feel her control slipping. Steve was so unpredictable; there was no telling just what he might do if pressed too far. 'But whatever it is it's just between the two of us.'

'Not when it involves Jill. Does it amuse you to show her how easily you can take Don from her?'

'No,' she denied heatedly. 'It doesn't amuse me at all. Can I help it that he happens to prefer me to your sister?'

'You can help encouraging him. On the face of it I'd say you'd been doing quite a bit of that.'

'On the face of it you'd probably say a whole lot of things without once hitting on the right version,' she came back with more spirit than organized thought. 'It wouldn't have occurred to you, I suppose, that I might have found myself in love with Don after all?'

There was a long pause before he answered that one, and when he did his voice had an odd note. 'No, it wouldn't. It wouldn't have occurred to me that you'd even know what love was about. I think you might be going through the same phase you went through with me.'

She stared at him, going first cold and then hot. 'You?'

'Yes.' His smile was mirthless. 'I was the first man you'd come into contact with apart from the station staff in over a year, and you were at an age when you were starting to need a little more than the reserve could offer. You enjoyed fighting with me, Sara. You even enjoyed losing to a certain extent. I represented the one thing lacking in your relationship with your father and Ted – sexual excitement. And there's no need to look like that. It's a perfectly natural emotion. Only don't confuse it with love.'

'I don't.' She was fighting now to save her pride, or the remnants of it. 'You're saying that I'm only attracted to Don because he's an extension of what I saw – if that's the right word – in you. Well, you know best how I feel, or felt about you, of course, but it doesn't have to follow that I haven't progressed since then. If there's one advantage Don does have over you it's in his integrity. He's never once kissed me against my will!'

Steve's lip curled deliberately and cruelly. 'Neither have I. You knew exactly what would happen that time – in fact you angled for it. If I'd chosen to I could have done anything I wanted with you at that moment.' He caught the hand which lifted involuntarily from her side, clasping it painfully in his own. 'It's a simple fact of life, kitten. Nothing to get worked up about. I just want you to realize that I have my own code of ethics, no matter what else you may have been thinking.'

Trembling, she tore herself free. 'One thing I have realized is that you're the most insufferably arrogant man I've ever met anywhere,' she spat at him. 'Don is worth three of you!'

'Is he?' There was a dangerous gleam in the grey eyes, a sudden tautening of the strong jawline. 'If that's your opinion it would seem that I've nothing to lose.'

His mouth and hands were brutal, without tenderness yet commanding a response. Sara made no attempt to fight him. She wasn't capable. She had asked for this too. He knew it and she knew it. When he finally let her go she couldn't look at him.

'I hate you,' she whispered quickly.

It was a moment before he said roughly, 'If it's any consolation I'm not over-enthusiastic about myself at the moment. One of these days you'll really make me hurt you, Sara, and then we'll both be sorry. Just accept that you're not going to get the better of me and stop trying, will you? I've had about as much as I can take. If Don is what you want then you have him.' He picked up his jacket which had fallen to the floor. 'Let's get back indoors.'

The others were still in the bar, and didn't appear to think they had been gone any undue length of time, although Sara thought that Diane gave her a rather narrow glance. She got through the rest of the evening somehow, dancing with Don, and once with Barry, but avoiding even an exchange of glances with Steve. Not that it was difficult. He had made his point and that was all he cared about. That was all he would ever care about where she was concerned. She put up a good pretence of not caring overmuch herself, laughing and sparkling as though she hadn't a problem in the world. It was only later in the privacy of her room that she could at last relax the pose and numbly acknowledge the fact that Steve had been right about one thing. She hadn't known what love was about. That was something she was only just beginning to learn, and it hurt like nothing had ever hurt before.

The week-end passed uneventfully. Sara had been hoping for a letter from her father on the Monday, but there was nothing in the main post, only a note from Ted brought in on the morning plane and delivered by hand from the Department offices.

Things had been pretty quiet since their departure, he said. Both Kiki and Mimi had missed her and fretted a little, but the monkey was as mischievous as ever, as no doubt Steve would have already informed her (Steve, thought Sara dryly, had had other things on his mind). Bruce Madden seemed fairly well recovered from the after-effects of his malaria, and welcomed the chance offered of spending the next week or so at Kambala before taking up a new post further north at Murchison Falls – a step up the ladder for him. For the rest, would she tell Steve that one of the patrols had turned up another gang of poachers over the week-end, and that there was a strong possibility of getting a lead on the organizers this time.

Steve received the news with the interest of one to whom the whole subject was of paramount importance, expressing the hope that with a bit of luck at least one illegal trading channel would shortly be shut off. Listening to him, Sara wondered how anyone as deeply involved as he was with the affairs of the Department could even contemplate giving it all up in favour of the kind of life led by the Milsons. So far nothing else had been said regarding the acquisition of the neighbouring farm, but the place was still on the market. Not that Steve would be content to leave the running of the place to a manager. Whatever he took on would receive his undivided attention.

Don took her out for a drive that afternoon, heading west along surfaced roads between the farms and plantations of Kikuyu country. The whole district seemed to be out on foot; they passed an unending procession of women carrying huge bulky burdens with the ease and poise of long custom, old men leading some domestic animal on a string, children, cattle, goats. This was the road which led eventually to Kambala, a hundred and ninety miles away, the road Sara hadn't travelled since the time over three years ago when her father had driven her overland to the station in order to show her the changing aspects as civilization was left behind. Perhaps they could return this way again when he came home next week, she thought with a pang of nostalgia for times past and gone. It would be nice to try and recapture some of the excitement and enthusiasm of her sixteen-year-old self.

'Why did you go in for farming, Don?' she asked at one point when they had paused to allow a meandering herd of goats go by.

'I didn't,' he replied. 'It was a proviso in my father's will that we continued to work the farm and live there for at least nine months of every year – or that one of us did.'

'Then it wouldn't have altered anything if Diane had gone to live somewhere else when you got married?'

'No.' He gave her a glance. 'Does it bother you that I've been married?'

Sara kept her expression unrevealing. 'Not at all. I just wonder sometimes what she was like, that's all.'

'Dark,' he said. 'Small, dark and vivacious. She was

twenty to my twenty-four when we met, and we had just over a year together before she left me.'

'I suppose,' Sara said carefully, 'that she liked a fairly lively time at that age?'

'She was a very lively person, and popular. Trouble was that she was jealous to death of Diane, couldn't bear her to get the attention at our gatherings. The man she eventually ran off with was one Diane thought quite a bit of herself. I often wonder if she did it because she really loved him, or just to prove to herself that she could take him from Di.'

'Did she marry him?'

'I suppose so. I never bothered to find out. When the divorce was finalized she was living in Kampala.' Don put the car into gear and moved forward as the road ahead cleared, added steadily, 'And whatever Freudian notions are tumbling around under that urchin cut of yours I still deny encouraging Jill to fall for me. She may have a certain look of Caro, but I got over that a long time ago.'

'But you can't bring yourself to trust anyone as far again,' she reminded him softly.

'No,' he agreed, 'that's true.' And then on an altered note, 'I almost had myself convinced that I might until I saw your face when Steve put in his unexpected appearance on Saturday night. I was wrong about that too. You *are* in love with him.'

Her face burned. 'No!'

'At least pay me the compliment about being honest about it. I'm not in deep enough to be badly hurt.'

She was silent for a long moment, her throat tight. 'All right,' she said huskily at last. 'It's true. I didn't realize it myself until I saw him again.'

'You did, I think, but you were hiding from it.' His smile was wry. 'If wanting was having we'd all be rich. If it's any consolation, I don't think Diane is going to get him either.'

Sara sat very still. 'No?'

'No. There was a time when I thought she might be prepared to put up with a lot to be Mrs. Steve York, only having seen her reactions to his way of life I'd say that the concessions are going to have to come with him, if at all.'

'But he's already considering that place next to yours. Surely . . .'

'You mean Jill hopes he's considering it. She's the one who wants him to settle down. Personally, I can't see it happening. He's not the compromising type.'

Sara could agree with that, but found small comfort in the rest. Whether Steve eventually married Diane or not it could make little difference to her own standing in his esteem. No doubt he would be highly relieved when her father finally returned to take over the responsibility he seemed unable to relinquish with a clear conscience himself.

'You're a rather exceptional person, Don,' she said, low-toned. 'I can't think why it isn't you I feel this way about. There are times when I actually hate Steve.'

A smile touched his mouth. 'Probably because you're a lot like him. If he had any sense he'd see that you'd make him a perfect partner. Unfortunately it doesn't work that way.'

'No.' There was nothing to add to that.

It was late when they got back. Steve was on the

veranda with Diane, a glass in his hand. He watched the two of them get out of the car and mount the steps unsmilingly, ran a deliberate and jeering eye over Sara's scrap of a sundress and nodded towards an envelope lying on the table by his knee.

'That came in an hour ago.'

Sara had to lean across him to pick the cablegram up. She opened it quickly, smoothing out the folded sheet. When she at last looked up again they were all watching her with varying expressions. Steve asked the obvious question.

'What happened?'

'It's from my father.' Her voice was quiet and unemotional. 'He was married this morning, and intends to stay on in England. He wants me to join him there.'

In the silence which followed the flat announcement, Sara's eyes followed the flight of a swallowtail flitting from blossom to blossom of the jacaranda just below the veranda. She supposed they had butterflies in England, particularly in the country places like Benston. Unspoiled and unchanged, her father had said in his last letter, but unchanged from what? Neat meadows divided by equally neat rows of fencing and cropped by tidy herds of Jersey cows; a stream flowing busily beneath a hump-backed bridge into a village of stone-built cottages with roses round the doors. Sara had seen pictures like that of English villages, and thought how pretty it all looked – and how miniature. How could her father even bear to think about living in such confinement after knowing places like Mara!

Steve took the cable from her unresisting hand, read it through swiftly and looked back at her.

'He says letter already on the way.'

'Yes.' She moved to the nearest chair and sat down, caught Don's eye and made an effort to rationalize her thoughts. 'I wonder if the Department knows yet.'

'If he doesn't intend coming back here at all then I imagine he'll have done something about informing them,' Steve said dryly. 'Would you like me to check?'

'I don't think so. If his resignation hasn't reached them yet it would sound bad coming from you.' Sara still couldn't quite take it in. Kenya was her home. How was she going to leave it all behind? On the other hand, how could she possibly stay under the circumstances? She had no qualifications – none, at least, which could be of any help in finding a job open to women. She had to join her father. There was no other course to take. 'I suppose he'll want me to arrange to have our things cleared out of Kambala and sent on,' she added musingly.

'We'll have to wait and see what he has to say in his letter.' Steve sounded hard and cold. 'No doubt that will contain all your instructions.' He heaved himself to his feet. 'I have to go into town, so I'll call in at the sorting offices and find out if there's anything for you while I'm down there. See you in an hour or so.'

Diane watched him go with a rather odd expression on her face, met her brother's eyes and gave a faint shrug, then spoke to Sara for the first time since she had returned. 'You must stay on here, of course, until everything is settled. Did you have any idea at all that your father might be thinking of doing this?'

'He did mention the woman he's married in one of

160

his letters a couple of weeks ago,' Sara replied tone-lessly. 'She's someone he knew years ago before we came out to East Africa – a widow. It never occurred to me that he would stay there, though.'

'No? Well, some men will always put a woman first.' Diane got up, stretched and looked up at the sky. 'I'd say we're going to get some rain in the next hour. It's to be hoped that Barry has the sense to realize it too. They've taken a picnic into the hills.'

She was proved right some fifteen minutes later when the heavens opened. It was still coming down in a solid sheet when Steve returned from town, and the shoulders of his shirt were drenched in the short dash from car to porch. There were several letters in his hand, the top one of which he handed over to Sara. She looked at the British stamps and the postmark dated five days previously, and was grateful when both Steve and Don disappeared, leaving her to open the envelope and read the letter on her own.

*I never imagined that this could happen to me again,* her father had written. *Or that it could mean more to me than the life I've made for myself out there these last years. Molly would have come with me if I'd asked her, but she would have been making yet another sacrifice and it's high time someone made a few for her. I've always had happy memories of Benston, as you know, and as it isn't too far from Windsor I might even fix myself up with a job in the Safari Park there. Not quite Africa, of course, but an adequate substitute given other compensations. By the time you get this we'll be married. I shall send you a wire on the day because we both want you to have some share in it. Molly is looking forward to seeing you again after all these years; she always wanted a daughter.* There was a little more in the same vein, and then: *I have naturally informed the Department that I shan't be returning, and have arranged that the balance of my accrued leave should be taken as notice of termination. With regard to Kambala, you will be able to sort out what we'll want to keep and leave the rest for the new Warden, whoever he might be. It shouldn't take long, and you could probably be on your way here by the end of the month. Perhaps you'd like to come by sea and have a holiday while you're at it. Buy whatever you want for the trip. It's time you started taking an interest in clothes and things like that.*

Sara was sitting there with the letter still open in her hand when Steve came back into the room. He had changed his shirt and run a brush over his damp hair, which gleamed like polished teak as it caught a stray beam of sunlight pushing its way valorously through the cloud. He lit a cigarette before speaking, leaning against the wall near the veranda door.

'Well?' he said.

'I'm to take a sea trip to England and have a good time,' she told him evenly. 'If there's a plane going out to Mara tomorrow I'd be able to sort things out at Kambala while Bruce Madden is still there. I don't want to intrude on the new man – if they manage to find someone to take over from Bruce at such short notice.'

'They have.' His tone was steady. 'I shall be driving out myself at the week-end. You can come with me then. A few days won't make much difference.'

Sara stared at him, her throat aching. 'You don't waste much time, do you? Is that why you went into town, to make sure no one else pipped you at the post? You needn't have worried. Kambala is a bit too remote for popularity.'

'Stop jumping to conclusions. I've been asked to help out again, that's all. I might take it on long term, I might not. It all depends on how things pan out. The poaching situation is far too serious in that section to leave the place without a co-ordinator.'

How things panned out, Sara surmised, depended on Diane. The latter would obviously not consider living in so remote a spot as Kambala, but that wasn't to say that she might not eventually come round to considering a rather more favourable proposition. Meanwhile, Steve would sit it out at Kambala. Farming, it appeared, had quite definitely been ruled out. Sara couldn't blame him. After being used to the wide open spaces few men could settle themselves to rural occupations – with her father the possible exception.

'Sorry,' she said. 'I think I'm feeling a bit edgy.'

'Hardly surprising. Think you're going to like England?'

'Why not? My father's there.'

'Revealing true parental devotion.' He held up a hand as she opened her mouth to revile that statement. 'All right, so every man has a right to decide his own future. What I am arguing with is his way of doing it, leaving you to do all the clearing up over here.' He paused, drew on the cigarette, added casually, 'Have you thought about staying on in Kenya yourself?'

'Doing what?' she asked.

He shrugged. 'You could get a job. The Game Department might help out there.'

'Sitting in an office filling out forms?' She shook her head wryly. 'I'd suffocate.'

'There must be other things you could do.'

'I can't think of anything. Anyway . . .' she paused, looked down at her hands folded tightly in her lap . . . 'you don't have to feel responsible for me any more. Strictly speaking that ended when I came to Nairobi.'

'Not when it's friends of mine you're staying with. My involvement will end the day you get aboard that ship or plane, or whatever.' He moved abruptly. 'We'll leave for Mara on Friday morning. Before that I'll check on available berths towards the month end. That will give you over a week to sort things out at the station. Think it will be long enough?'

'Plenty.' She hardly knew what to say. 'I'll try not to get in your way.'

His smile was ironical. 'I'm sure you will.' There was the sound of a car outside and he came away from the wall. 'That will be Jill.'

It was. She came in laughing and soaked to the skin, Barry having carried on to his own house to change. They had been quite a distance from the car when the rain had started and within seconds had barely been able to see the vehicle through the deluge. Then the car had refused to start and they had been forced to sit there steaming in their wet clothes until the rain let up

164

enough to allow Barry to take a look under the bonnet.

There was a vast difference in the other girl's whole demeanour, thought Sara, viewing the sparkling eyes and healthily flushed cheeks. She was fast getting over Don, perhaps already quite free of any lingering feelings for the man she had believed herself in love with. Sara only wished she could teach herself to do the same.

# CHAPTER EIGHT

THEY left Kambala an hour after dawn on Friday, heading west along the road Sara had taken with Don a few days before. Jill and Don had both got up early to see them off, but Diane didn't bother to put in an appearance until the last moment, emerging from her room in a black and gold kimono-style wrap which suited her slender elegance.

At some time during the week it had been decided that she should accompany Jill down to Mombasa on the afternoon flight, although it was still uncertain as to how long the former intended to stay or what her particular purpose was in going. Privately Sara wondered if she was trying to show Steve that she would not be content to sit around waiting for him for ever by implying that there were other attractions down at the coast. If that was it she could have gained small satisfaction from Steve's reactions, as he appeared totally unmoved. It was probably a case, thought Sara, of who would break first. Somehow she doubted that it would be Steve. No matter how much he might want Diane he would never allow a woman to dictate terms in that way.

He didn't seem disposed for conversation during the first part of the journey. In no state of mind for idle chat herself, Sara kept her attention on the passing scenery, only too conscious that she was seeing it for the last time. A passage was booked for her on a ship leaving Mombasa in a week's time. On the day before that she was to fly direct from Mara to the port, and spend a night with Jill before embarking. Between then and now stretched a no-man's-land she didn't even want to consider for the moment.

She wondered how Ted had taken the news of his old friend's desertion, and whether he would be staying on under Steve's direction if the latter eventually decided to keep the job for a while. Kambala had been Ted's home for more than ten years. Sara couldn't see him wanting to pull up roots at this state of his life, yet she knew that Steve had often been impatient of the older man's somewhat happy-go-lucky attitude to life and work. Ted and her father had got along because in many ways they were alike, but it was doubtful that Steve would be willing to put up with the same way of things for very long. He wasn't the kind to allow sentiment to colour his judgment.

Gradually the farms were left behind, replaced by fenced ranches and then eventually the open uplands beyond the Great Rift Valley with their view of far distant mountains. Wild life began to appear upon the scene: giraffe, antelope, the occasional small herd of zebra grazing peacefully, and once a sounder of warthogs trotting away into the grass, tails rigidly erect. They made a brief stop for a packed lunch of cold meat and fruit about one, and by two had reached the trading post, which was Narok, the last settlement of any kind between here and Kambala.

There was a small group of Masai sitting on the grass outside the store happily sorting cowrie shells. Steve stopped to greet them, shaking hands solemnly through the opened window, responding to the warmth and smiling gaiety of these people to whom Mara was home. By the time they were on their way again he seemed to have relaxed from the phlegmatic stranger of the morning to something approaching affability.

'Not long now,' he commented when they were inside the gates of the reserve. 'Another couple of hours should see us through.' He glanced round when he received no answer. 'Tired?'

'A bit,' she acknowledged. 'It will be nice to get home . . .' She stopped abruptly, chopping off the end of the word. 'There,' she amended.

'It's still home until you've actually moved out,' Steve returned evenly. 'And for today at least we're not going to give that another thought. I hope Maswi is having one of his good days, or I suppose it will be fish balls and curry for dinner.'

Sara laughed. 'Left to him it would be that all the time. They're easiest to manage. I don't think it's that he's lazy exactly, just that their own diet is monotonous and he simply can't see the reason why we should be so mad keen on variety. I hope they stay out the full six months for you, but I have my doubts. They're both eager to see their families again.'

'They're wanting their women,' he said bluntly. 'Hardly surprising. A pity there's nowhere handier we could recruit our domestic staff from.'

The road dwindled to little more than a track and dropped to run along the foot of the Escarpment. From here the plains stretched for ever, a golden sea rolling southwards, forming shifting patterns in the wind. The sun was slanting fast by the time they reached the river, the Escarpment behind them dark and forbidding against the bank of cloud piling up from the east. Then they were through the trees and Kambala lay before them, unchanged and familiar.

Ted came round the corner of the house as they drew up in front.

'Good journey?' he asked.

'So-so.' Steve got out and stretched his arms, lifted an inquiring eyebrow in Sara's direction as she came round the bonnet. 'Drink?'

She shook her head. 'I'd rather get cleaned up first.'

'I'll get your bags out. Ted can give me a hand with the rest of the stuff later.'

It was Ted who brought her cases along to her room some few minutes later, hoisting them on to the bed and standing back to grin at her cheerfully.

'Time was when you could have got all your stuff in a small size grip,' he remarked. 'Been learning how the other half lives at last?'

'You might say that.' Her smile lacked sparkle, and she saw his eyes narrow thoughtfully. Hastily she changed the subject. 'Have you decided what you're going to do yet, Ted?'

His shrug was careless, but she knew him too well to be fully deceived. 'Depends on the boss. We haven't always seen eye to eye this last few weeks, and you need harmony to live in a place like this. I might mosey down to the coast and pick up a cheap boat, do a bit of trading round the ports. There's money to be made in that game if you play your cards right.'

'You've always been a land man,' she exclaimed.

'You don't know anything about the sea!'

'I don't need to know about it to chug along the coastline, and I've plenty of experience in trading, even if I am a bit out of touch. I'll manage.'

A bit out of touch was an understatement, thought Sara when he had gone. He never seemed to spend much on himself so it was more than possible that he had enough put by to buy himself the boat he had spoken of, but she was quite sure the rest of his so-called plan had been a spur-of-the-moment idea to waylay her fears. Her lips firmed suddenly. Ted couldn't be allowed to leave the only real home he knew, and Steve must be made to see it. He must!

Kiki appeared at the open window chattering wildly. Next moment Sara had her hands and arms full of monkey as the animal launched itself across the intervening space to cling like a limpet to her shirt. Laughing, she collapsed on the bed, fending him off as best she could until his excess of zeal had exhausted itself and he sprang away to curiously examine the contents of her shoulder bag which had spilled out on to the spread.

Watching him handle a lipstick case with frowning intensity she realized for the first time that Kiki was one of the things she was going to have to leave behind when she went to England. Even if it were allowed, she could hardly take a monkey on board ship with her for such a length of time, to say nothing of the difference in English climate. Tears prickled behind her eyelids and she blinked rapidly to disperse them. It was no use giving way to emotionalism; she was going, and that was that. For the coming two weeks she must put a brave face on it and pretend that it didn't matter to her, because she couldn't bear to have Steve know how she really felt. He was too astute, too capable of realizing that Kambala wasn't the only reason she so desperately wanted to stay in Kenya. He might have been aware of his attraction for her in the first place, but he had made it clear that he had no suspicion at all of any deeper involvement. She intended to keep it that way.

Maswi was apparently in one of his better moods, and had excelled himself by producing a very fair meat pie garnished with bright green peas and asparagus from the stores they had brought through with them from Nairobi, followed by fruit flan and cream. Steve opened a couple of bottles of wine in celebration, suggested brandy with the coffee and expressed the hope that fish balls and curry had been stricken from the menu permanently.

'You might get around to making out a list of dishes he can manage as easily,' he suggested to Sara. 'It would make life round here infinitely more worth living.'

'I hadn't realized you were all that interested in food, providing there was enough of it,' she responded. 'Neither Dad or Ted seem to care what they eat.'

'Beggars can't be choosers,' remarked the latter on a dry note. He pushed his cup to one side and got up, looking suddenly old and tired. 'Hope nobody minds if I turn in early.'

There was a long pause after he had gone. Sara lay with her head against the back of her chair, eyes on the stars which gleamed fitfully between the patches of cloud. The baboons were having a field day, their anguished barks drowning out most other sounds. Yet even they could not disturb the particular quality of peace which lay in the high plains. Nairobi had been enjoyable, and she had learned a great deal about herself, but nothing could touch this sense of belonging, of completeness. Eventually her feelings for Steve must start to fade, but no matter where she went a part of her would always remain here at Kambala.

'More brandy?' he asked, and she started, coming out of her reverie to find him holding out the bottle towards the glass she had been unconsciously twisting between her fingers.

'No, thanks,' she said quickly. 'I think I've had enough. Between the coffee and the brandy I doubt that I'll sleep much as it is.'

'It's barely ten,' he came back. 'You've time to get over both.' He surveyed her slender form stretched in the chair. 'I half expected you to go back to your old habits now that there's no one around to impress.'

Something in his tone hardened her. She answered lightly, 'Habits change more easily than people, I've found. I got used to wearing a dress in the evening. It's as simple as that.'

His mouth became sardonic. 'With you nothing is simple. Not these days. There was a time when you were fairly straightforward, before you learned civilized ways. Now, you're like all the rest of your sex.'

'Well, I should hope so!'

'I wasn't referring to your physical attributes.' His gaze slid over her again, this time with cool deliberation. 'Although you're in no way lacking in that department either, as I should know.' He watched the warmth rise in her cheeks mercilessly. 'Nice to know you haven't become blasé about everything.'

'Did you say something about civilized ways?' she queried in a tight little voice. 'You've obviously been out of contact too long yourself.'

'You could be right. Which makes me an uncertain bet in the predictability stakes.' He half raised his glass to her mockingly. 'Peace.'

That they would never have, she thought. Not for long, at any rate. They seemed to have proved it these last few minutes. Whenever they talked together the same thing happened, the same ding-dong battle. She wasn't sure whose fault it was, or even that it mattered. They were incompatible, and that was that.

'What are you going to do about Ted?' she asked into the pause, and then caught at her lip with her lower teeth, wondering what on earth had prompted her to bring that subject up at such a time. She hadn't meant to say it; it had just come out.

Steve's expression was unhelpful. 'What am I supposed to be going to do about him?'

Having begun it she had to continue. 'He thinks you might be intending to replace him.'

'Does he?' He poured himself another brandy, re-stopped the bottle and lifted the glass again. 'Are you supposed to plead his cause for him?'

She caught back the heated retort. 'No, I'm not. He wouldn't ask anyone to do that. I simply thought that he was entitled to know where he stood.'

'He is.' His voice was deceptively quiet. 'You're not – until he can tell you himself.'

He was in the right, of course, and knowing it didn't

help at all. She hadn't studied that particular aspect of the matter, but jumped in as usual with both feet. 'I'll try to remember,' she said coolly, and pressed herself up from the chair. 'I'm sure you won't mind if I leave you. After all, you do have the rest of the brandy for company.'

She was half-way to the door when he said her name in a voice which was quiet but authoritative enough to halt her footsteps and turn her slowly back to look at him. His own eyes were on the glass in his hand, his mouth a taut line.

'There's a limit to all feats of endurance,' he said without moving. 'And you've almost reached it. I thought there was a chance that we might come to understand one another this next week; right now it seems a pretty remote one. Perhaps if you stopped trying to see a personal slight in everything I say we'd do better.'

Sara swallowed thickly, fighting the overwhelming longing to throw caution to the winds and go to him, to lay her head against his chest and beg him to let her stay. How could he hope to understand her when she didn't even understand herself? She loved him, yet overriding that was this need to reach out and hurt. Civilized. Compared with the human race the wild life out there were streets ahead.

'I think you were right the first time,' she heard herself saying with a sense of fatalistic acceptance. 'The chance seems remote.'

He made no answer as she went on indoors.

By morning Sara had reached a decision. The way things were between her and Steve another week would be hard to take. If she set about it with a will she could easily get things sorted out in a few days, and then there would be nothing to keep her here. There was still a fair amount of cash in her name at the bank in Nairobi – enough to keep her in a hotel until the ship sailed. And it could only be a relief to Steve to have her out of his hair at last.

Not that she had any intention of telling him of her change in plans – or anyone else, for that matter. He would only try to stop her. No, she had to plan this very carefully and secretly if she wanted to succeed. And she had to succeed. She had to get away before she gave herself away. She could bear anything but that.

Steve had already left when she got outside, but Ted joined her for a cup of coffee from her fresh pot. He looked infinitely more cheerful this morning, almost his old self.

'You've got into bad habits while you've been away,' he commented. 'Normally you'd have been up and about a couple of hours or more before this.'

'I was tired,' she said. 'The journey yesterday, plus too many late nights, I suppose.' She eyed him speculatively across the table. 'Have you thought any more about what you were telling me last night?'

He shook his head, and grinned. 'Seems I was crossing my bridges before I came to them. The way Steve was talking this morning he's counting on my being around for some time yet. Maybe we'll hit things off better now that he's not a temp any more.'

But he is, Sara started to say, then caught herself up. She didn't know, did she? Steve himself wasn't sure yet. She wondered if he had allotted himself a certain time lapse before he made any move towards Diane again, or whether he would simply sit back and wait for her to contact him before deciding on what extent of compromise he was prepared to offer her. She thought probably the latter. His kind of male pride would never sink below a certain level.

She made a start on packing immediately after breakfast, getting Njorogi to bring in a couple of packing cases to the living-room to hold her father's books and personal papers. By midday the shelves were bare and the room was beginning to look denuded with its walls shorn of the few prints hung there over the years in occasional attempts to brighten up the place. She couldn't imagine Molly having any use for half a dozen worn skin rugs, so she left them where they were together with the curtains and cushion covers. She wasn't sure yet where they would all eventually be living, but wherever it was such items would more than likely have been provided long before she got home. In any case, she couldn't leave the *banda* completely cheerless.

She was on her knees sorting through the pile of records when Steve came back at four. He stopped in the doorway to run his eyes over the already filled crates, mouth cynical.

'Great little worker, aren't you?' he said. 'Maybe we should keep you here after all. What are you going to do for the rest of the week?'

'I haven't finished yet,' she answered without looking up. 'Would you like the record player? It's a relic, but at least it works.'

'Sure. Why not? It will help to fill the gap when Ted

and I run out of conversation.' He moved across and helped himself to whisky, added without turning his head, 'The tribe are getting ready to move out in the morning. If you like I'll run you over later on to say good-bye to Mgari and his wives.'

Sara sat back on her heels heavily. It was all coming to an end at once. Somehow that seemed fitting. The Masai belonged to a chapter in her life which she would never forget; she wanted to remember them as she had last seen them on the night of the *ngoma*.

'They don't like good-byes,' she said.

'Suit yourself.' From his tone he couldn't have cared less whether she went or not. He had made the gesture and that let him out. He finished his drink and left her there.

By Sunday night Sara had done all that she needed to do. The crates were packed and labelled ready for Friday's plane out, and her own plans were made. That they involved leaving the station short of a vehicle had been a matter for some concern at first, but with Kimani gone she felt that the remaining three cars should suffice for a few days. She refused to even consider the fact that someone was going to have to drive back the car she herself was borrowing. It was the only way she had of getting away before the week-end, so that was that. It was simply unfortunate that the Department should have to be put to any trouble because of her.

The evening seemed unbearably long. After dinner Sara made an attempt to interest herself in a book, but the words kept jumping up and down in front of her eyes. She could hear the murmur of voices as the two men talked out on the veranda, but couldn't bring herself to join them for fear of betraying herself by some word or gesture. This was the last time she would ever sit like this in this room, the last time she would ever hear the familiar sounds of the night floating in out of the darkness out there. By this time tomorrow she would be back in Nairobi, alone in a hotel bedroom with four more days to get through somehow. But anything was better than staying on here right now. Anything at all!

Steve came in some minutes later to refill both glasses. He glanced at her briefly in passing, but made no comment until he was putting the bottle back again.

'What about the dik-dik?' he asked abruptly. 'Do you want me to have it shipped out to a zoo?'

She looked up in dismay. 'You wouldn't do that!'

'I might not have a choice. It's still too young to be turned loose, and I'm not at all sure that it would work now, anyway. You've made it too dependent on you, too used to human company. It's always a mistake to allow wild animals to become attached. You should have known that.'

'Why can't she just stay here on the station?' she asked on a faintly tremulous note. 'She wouldn't be any trouble. Ted would take care of her.'

His lips firmed. 'Ted has enough to do without looking after your menagerie. The monkey is bad enough, but at least he can fend for himself.'

'One tiny fawn isn't going to disrupt his work schedule all that much.' She laid the book down on the arm of her chair and sat looking at it for a moment before saying in a low tone, 'Do you want me to plead with you, Steve? Is that it?'

'It would be a novelty,' he answered with satire. 'Sara Macdonald brought to her knees at last! It's quite a thought, but not, as it happens, what I'm after. It's the animal I'm thinking of.'

Her eyes came up then and met his, one pair bright, blazing blue, the other cool, grey and unreadable. 'Then you must do as you think best,' she said with forced steadiness. 'Strictly speaking it's no longer my concern. Was there anything else you wanted to discuss?'

A muscle jerked suddenly in his jaw; he took a single step towards her, then checked, lip curling. 'Oh no, you don't! I'm not rising to that again. From now on you can play your vicious little games elsewhere! Only make sure you choose your partners very carefully, kitten, or one of these fine days you're going to get just what you're asking for!'

Sara didn't move as he picked up the glasses and walked past her out on to the veranda again. She felt deadly tired and more than a little sick. Tomorrow couldn't come soon enough!

It rained heavily during the night, but the morning was fine and dry with a delicious freshness in the air. Sara waited with deliberation until Steve was out of the way before emerging from her room, listening to the dying sound of his engine with a complete lack of emotion of any kind.

Ted was already about his business. She ate a solitary breakfast, not in the least bit hungry but conscious of the fact that it would be the last food she would get until the evening, apart from a couple of packets of chocolate and some fruit. She didn't want to risk being seen taking food from the kitchen in case either of the two houseboys took it into their heads to mention it to Ted before she was away. The thought of the long drive ahead didn't worry her too much, although it would certainly be the longest period she had ever spent behind the wheel. Once she got to Narok the going would be fairly easy.

The Land-Rover she had chosen to take was the one parked right down near the top of the track. At a little after eight-thirty, after having made sure that Ted was well out of earshot in the rear sheds, she made her way out to it cautiously, carrying the single suitcase which contained all her immediate personal needs. With that stacked in the back and the tail gate up, there was still plenty of room to spread the piece of blanket for the fawn. She went and fetched it quickly, pressing her cheek to the smooth coat as she lifted it into the car. What she was going to do with the little animal when she got to Nairobi she still wasn't at all certain, but it would not be going to any zoo. Perhaps Don would help her out. There was plenty of room at the farm for a young antelope to grow in freedom and safety, and as Steve had said, it was quite accustomed to human contact.

There was no one around when she finally climbed behind the wheel. Neither did anyone appear when she started the engine and headed for the gates. Not that it would have mattered so much at this point. Even if Ted had seen her setting off he would more than likely have assumed that she was kicking over the traces again to go out alone on to the reserve. He would only know the truth when he eventually went into his own room and saw the letter she had propped up on his pillow. If there was one thing Sara really regretted about this whole affair it was not being able to say good-bye properly to the man she had been so fond of all these years, but that was impossible. If he had any idea at all of her intentions he wouldn't hesitate to call Steve in to stop her.

She avoided looking in the mirror until she swung the wheel to enter the trees which shut off all sight of Kambala.

It took her well over an hour to reach the Escarpment. By then the sun was high in the sky and it was already growing uncomfortably warm in the car. Sara stopped for a few minutes to give the fawn a drink from the flask she had brought with her, pouring a small amount of water into the cupped palm of her hand and holding it out to the long black muzzle. If she could keep up round about the same speed she should make Nairobi just before dark, she reckoned. That was always providing she met with no unforeseen difficulties. It meant that when she did get there she would have the choice of either going straight out to the farm with the fawn, or leaving it in the car overnight outside whichever hotel she stayed in. A decision she would make when she eventually got there, she decided after a moment or two.

She had been going another forty minutes or so when she first noticed the dust cloud far back on the track behind her. Whatever was coming was coming fast, driven furiously without regard to springs or shock-absorbers. With her heart thudding sickeningly into her throat, Sara put her own foot down, watching the needle swing up to the forty mark and hover there. It could only be Steve in the car behind her. No one else would risk that speed on a dirt road.

He was overtaking her – there was no doubt about that. In the few moments which had passed since she had first spotted the following car he had closed the gap between them by several miles. She increased her own speed again, hardly knowing what she hoped to achieve by running away from him miles from anywhere, only conscious of the need to keep as much distance as possible between them. Whatever happened, she thought wildly, she would not go back. She had finished with that part of her life for ever!

Despite all her efforts the other car gradually crept closer, hidden at times by bends in the track, but always that bit nearer when it appeared again. Soon Sara could see the man behind the wheel through her mirror, although he was still too far away as yet to make out any expression. Not that she needed any confirmation.

Something had to happen, of course, and when it did it happened quickly. Rounding a particularly tight corner, Sara found herself almost on top of a troop of baboons scattered across the track. Instinctively she slammed on the brakes and swerved with a screaming of tortured rubber, heading straight for the belt of trees and bush which came almost down to the road at this point. There was a heart-stopping moment when she was sure that she wasn't going to be able to avoid a collision, then her front wheel hit a boulder hidden in the long grass, and the whole side lifted to teeter sickeningly on the brink of overturning for an interminable second before crashing down again with a jolt which shook every bone in her body and tore the wheel from her grasp. But at least she had stopped.

The baboons had vanished into the trees by the time the other car came round the bend. Steve drew to a skidding halt and leaped out, striding across the grass to where Sara sat waiting. His face was tight, his eyes chips of grey ice.

'What are you trying to do, kill yourself?' he demanded, taking in the damage in one sweeping glance. 'It's a wonder you didn't overturn taking a bend like that at the speed you were travelling!'

'You shouldn't have chased me.' Her voice was astonishingly steady, Sara noted with oddly detached interest. 'And you were moving even faster than I was when you came round that bend.'

'I kept control of the car,' he pointed out grimly. 'I'm not prepared to stand about arguing about it either.' He moved to the back end, his mouth hardening even further when he saw the fawn cowering down scared half out of its wits. 'Come and get a hold of this and put it in the back of mine. I'll bring your case.'

'I'm not going back to Kambala with you,' she stated flatly, and saw his eyes spark dangerously.

'No?'

'No.' The detachment was fading fast, feeling flowing back into her numbed senses. This time her voice shook just a little. 'I – I won't go through another four days like the last two. I don't have to, and I won't! The car isn't badly damaged. I can carry on from here.'

'To what?' he demanded. 'Don?'

'Oh, be damned to Don!' she burst out in a sudden upsurge of fury. 'I couldn't care less if I never saw him again either! I'm going to Nairobi because I can't stand being in the same house with you any longer, because I'm sick and tired of being treated like some silly little teenager who isn't even capable of knowing her own mind! You've done nothing but push me around since that very first day – and make fun of me.' There was no holding the torrent of words, they were spilling from her like a dam bursting its banks. 'I pity Diane if she ever marries you. I really do! Not that I think you have a chance. She's too independent a person to subjugate herself to your kind of tyranny! I hope she finds someone else while she's down at the coast. A man capable of some real feeling. You couldn't feel deeply about anything or anyone if you tried! All you want is for everyone to toe the line: Yes, Steve; no, Steve; three bags full, Steve!' She was begining to sound ridiculous; she knew it, and still she couldn't make herself stop. 'You don't want a wife, you want a doormat!'

'You're starting to repeat yourself,' he said mildly, and she looked at him sharply. A complete change had come over his expression. His lips were twitching, his eyes glinting with laughter. 'Nice to have the original model back. Now we all know where we stand.'

Colour swept into her face, then out again as swiftly. She had given herself away for certain this time. Steve knew, and was amused by the knowledge. She turned away.

'Go away,' she said thickly. 'Just go away and leave me alone.'

'After getting this far?' He was behind her, turning her, holding her relentlessly there in front of him. 'What makes you think it's Diane I want?'

Sara stared back at him blankly, her mind refusing to take in the implications. 'It's . . . obvious,' she managed.

'Not to me it isn't. How could I think about her with you driving me half round the bend?' His voice was forceful. 'You've got me so that I can't even concentrate on my work any more. That's why I turned back this morning, to sort things out between us. When Ted found your letter I didn't stop to think at all, just jumped in the car and came after you. You're not going to England, Sara. Not until we can both go together.'

A curious light-headedness had come over her. 'I'm not?'

'No. You're going to stay on at Kambala and get to know me better. I'm aware that you're only on the verge of what I feel about you, but I can do something about that.' His gaze kindled suddenly as he looked down into her stunned blue eyes. 'Starting now. Like this.'

Sara came back to life as his mouth touched hers, and this time there was no holding back. When he finally held her away from him she was glowing and breathless and at last beginning to believe what she meant to him.

'Why didn't you tell me before?' she asked. 'You've been so . . . so cruel these last few days.'

'I should think so too!' He was still holding her in his arms, searching her face with an odd expression. 'I couldn't fathom you any more, couldn't tell what you were thinking or feeling. I tried everything I knew to get through that skin you'd acquired while you were in Nairobi and find the real Sara again, but I couldn't seem to hit the right spark.' He paused. 'Maybe I've been using the wrong tactics all along the line. Maybe I could have saved us both a lot of trouble if I'd used a more physical approach on Friday night. Sara, what I said just now about you only just beginning to feel something for me . . .'

'You were wrong about that too,' she said softly. 'I'm just as capable as you of experiencing emotions. I love you, Steve, and I *do* know what it means. I've known for at least a week. So you'd better stop thinking of me as young Sara from now on and start treating me like a real woman for a change.'

'I stopped thinking of you as young Sara the night I came to the club with Diane and saw you with Don,' he answered on a slightly rough note. 'You looked anything but a kid right then.'

'Is that when you began . . . well, feeling the way you do about me now?'

He laughed softly. 'That's when I began admitting it. You've always been the most tantalizing, infuriating, impossible-to-ignore female I ever came across, only I wouldn't let myself see beyond the fact that you were only Jill's age, and had missed out on so much. I suppose that should still concern me, but I'm not going to let it. How do you feel about marrying a tyrant yourself?'

'I think I could learn to handle it,' she said demurely. 'When?'

'As soon as we can arrange it.' He looked into her upturned face and made a sound like a groan. 'For God's sake don't look at me like that or I'll not be answerable for the consequences! Just remember that repression is bad for the health, and try not to put too much temptation my way this next few days, will you?' He kissed her again once, then put her firmly from him. 'Let's get on the way. I'll send a couple of the boys out for your car.'

Between them they transferred both suitcase and fawn to the back of the other Rover, then got into the cabin themselves. Sara turned her head to look at the vital features of the man sitting beside her in the driving seat, met the smiling grey regard and felt her heart turn over in pure, exhilarating happiness. Steve was taking her home again. And this time it was for good.

Be sure always to look for the name MILLS & BOON on the covers, so that you may be certain the books are genuine MILLS & BOON publications. In case of difficulty in obtaining the books – or if you would like us to send you post free our catalogue – please write to us:

**MILLS & BOON READER SERVICE**

P.O. BOX 236

14 SANDERSTEAD ROAD

S. CROYDON CR2 0YG, SURREY

ENGLAND

Will SOUTH PACIFIC readers please write to:

**MILLS & BOON READER SERVICE**

P.O. BOX 958

NORTH SYDNEY

N.S.W. 2060

474